Love Floats

by

D. W. Thompson

An Emma Love Mystery

Love Floats

Cover Art by *Lea Schizas*

The Wild Rose Press, Inc.
PO Box 708
Adams Basin, NY 14410-0708
Visit us at www.thewildrosepress.com

Publishing History
First Edition, 2025
Trade Paperback Print ISBN 978-1-5092-6411-7
Digital ISBN 978-1-5092-6412-4

An Emma Love Mystery
Published in the United States of America

Dedication

To my ever-understanding wife, Terry, my ever-encouraging editor, Lea, my ever-supportive family, and my ever-faithful readers, thank you as always from my heart.

Chapter One

I stretched to lift the first of the four kayaks we'd take out on the Bay this evening. My twelve-foot kayak was already moored at the water's edge. This was to be the inaugural moonlight float for my company, Love's Kayaking Floats, and Tours. My clients and fellow paddle enthusiasts were scheduled to arrive on site within the next half hour. The full moon reflected off the mirrored surface of the bay. Despite the fog moving in, it promised to be a perfect night for a float.

I pulled four additional life vests from the Amish-built shed I'd bought over the winter, then grabbed another four whistles and paddles. That took care of the hardware. I pulled a bungee cord tight over the small cooler with bottled water, and we were ready to go.

After the fight with Sam just hours before, I needed this jaunt into tranquil waters—no pun intended. My winter of discontent was over. Spring was in the air. I was glad I had my private investigator's license to fill in for kayaking's dead season. It helped to pay the bills, but Sam couldn't understand that I needed a reprieve from cheating husbands and wives. I needed time in nature, floating in the river, and tending my vegetable garden.

I hoped my companions this evening agreed with my way of thinking. Some customers chatted non-stop during our trips. Others completed the entire journey with a set of earphones plugged in, often at a volume so loud it distracted the whole group and defeated the purpose. But I still considered it a success if they enjoyed the journey.

I knew only one of my guests this evening. Katrina Baker was an old friend, or at least as close as I got to one in high school, even though she was a year ahead of me. Back then, the teenage boys called her a bombshell. Her long, bottle-blonde hair and shapely figure got her out of as many jams as they got her into. Katrina opened a bakery about the same time I returned home and just after her divorce. The rumor was that her husband had found someone younger in the next county.

I guess the bakery was preordained, considering Katrina's last name. Her Maple and Main Street corner sign read Baker's Bakery Shop. They made the best donuts in town. Kat was bringing her younger sister along on their first kayaking adventure. I wasn't surprised that I didn't remember her. Upperclassmen tend to overlook students in the lower grades. Sofia was two years behind me. The last two ladies joining us were one of Sofia's old classmates, who was home for a visit, and one of her friends.

As I slid the last kayak into the water and tied it by the launch, a set of headlights pulled into my driveway. I couldn't tell what kind of vehicle it was. The moon was full, but the fog was thick. The mist between me and the car appeared to engulf me.

"Hey, Emma. Do you need some help?" Katrina yelled.

"No, I think I'm good." I heard three separate car doors slam—but I could only discern ghostly figures

2

drifting toward me through the mist.

"You don't think some hot-rod teenager will run us over in a powerboat out there, do you?" she asked.

"We'll stay close to shore in the shallows, Kat. I'm going into the house for a moment to grab some lights. You ladies can unload any gear you have. Pick out your kayak and ensure your life vests fit. Katrina said you were all young and skinny."

"Maybe them. I'm sure I didn't say that about myself." Katrina laughed.

"No worries, they are adjustable," I said. "You're going to bake in that thick sweatshirt, Kat. It's only dropping down to sixty-five degrees or so by the time we get back."

"I don't like to be cold," she answered.

"Okay, I warned you. But wasn't there a fourth lady coming?"

"Our other friend has been out of touch. I don't think she will make it."

"Shame, but that's fine. Give me a minute, and I'll be right back. There's one more thing we need."

I trotted toward the house, and Sam opened the door as I approached.

"I just finished my report on the 'snatch and grab' at the supermarket. Looks like I'm too late to help with the kayaks though,"

"No worries. The ladies could use your help pulling them out when we return though,"

"You sure you want to go out in this? The fog is getting thick, and the temperature is supposed to drop around midnight."

"We'll be fine. You know I've done this a hundred times. I could paddle to River's End and back blindfolded."

"You have your phone, just in case?"

"I do. Don't worry. We should be back in about two hours. Some of the women haven't kayaked before. I don't want to push them too much on their first outing. Plus, we'll be hanging close to the shoreline."

With the flashlights in hand, I hugged Sam. "See you soon."

"Make sure you do. Be safe out there."

"Maybe you'll join me sometime."

"I'm strictly a landlubber, Emma, but I may have to learn so I can keep up with you."

When I walked down the bank to the Bay, my kayakers were already sitting in their kayaks at the water's edge.

"Ready to go, I see."

"We are," Katrina said. "Oh, Emma, where are my manners? You remember my sister, Sofia, right?"

"Sure, I remember her," I lied. "How have you been, Sofia?" She was a thin woman with a pixie-cut. The color varied with flashes of pink, blue, and fluorescent green.

"Great. A little nervous about tipping over tonight, but otherwise, I'm good. We studied the brochure you gave Katrina, and I think we have the paddling strokes down. This is my old friend Valerie. She lives in New York now but gets home occasionally, and we have a girls' night out without my kids or hubby when she does."

"I'm pleased to meet you, Valerie," I said, and we shook hands.

"It's just Val, Emma. Do you have any tips on how not to fall out of this boat? No, don't laugh. I'm serious."

"I know, and you'd be amazed how often I'm asked that. Stay in the center of the kayak. Don't lean out over the sides. This is flat water, Val. You don't need any fancy strokes here. Paddle only on the left, and you'll turn right and vice versa. If you want to turn fast, stick your paddle straight down, and you'll turn in that direction. It's a relaxing float. You'll see."

I put a flashlight under the bungee straps at the front of each woman's kayak.

"Just an added safety measure," I assured them. With that, we paddled out into the bay.

Katrina and Sofia mastered the paddling with minimal effort. Valerie started well until she turned in a big circle, and her kayak headed back toward the bank.

"Even strokes, Val. One side and then the other."

She was a quick learner, and we floated past the first inlet creek and beyond. An owl released its eerie purring trill followed by a whinnying sound, not unlike a ghostly and demented colt.

"What the heck was that?" Sofia asked. "It sounded like the Headless Horseman's beast."

"It's a screech owl. We hear them a lot at night," I answered.

"Maybe that's what you need as a partner for your private investigations, Emma. He could do all the late-night stakeouts," Katrina said.

"That's a great idea. I wonder if he works cheap?"

"I could use him at the bakery shop too."

"I'm not sure that old Mister Owl would make a very good taste tester."

"No—not for that. Didn't Sam tell you? I had a break-in the night before last. It didn't look like they took much. I had a little money in the cash register because there wasn't enough to make a night drop at the bank worthwhile. I'd taken the money to the bank at lunchtime, and most of my business is in the mornings."

"That's terrible, Kat. What did the sheriff's office say?"

"They think it was kids. I know my insurance will cover the tab for the broken door glass and the smashed cash register, but what if I had worked late that night? I do sometimes so I can get an early start on the donuts for the morning rush. I had to take Harper to her high school for their night volleyball game, though. Guess I was lucky."

"Little Harper is in high school now?"

"Little Harper is fourteen and going on thirty. She's a sophomore, but she made the varsity team this year. She scares me, Emma. She looks every bit of twenty-one and thinks she is too." Katrina must have noticed the look in my eyes and realized I was doing the mental math.

"Remember, I started young and was held back in the first grade." She laughed and wiggled in her seat.

"You sure did. I remember." I nodded.

"Look, Emma. I need to take a Mother Nature break. Sorry. I drank about a half-gallon of sweet tea before I left—like a dummy. Is this a good spot to get out? Is the bank dry?"

"Should be fine, and there are no venomous snakes, or poison ivy vines this time of year."

"That's good to know. You guys go ahead. I'll catch up. I can paddle circles around those two young'uns anyway."

6

"Haha, so not funny," Sofia said.

We paddled on for five minutes until we neared the last inlet before the River's End housing development. I turned around but still couldn't see Katrina. Sofia noticed.

"Shouldn't she at least be out on the water by now, Emma?"

"I'm not sure, Sofia. Is she one of those who take Dostoevsky's "War and Peace" to read in the bathroom?" I asked, joking for my client's sake, but I also felt some concern. I shouldn't have let her leave the group.

"We'll give her five more minutes. If she is still a no-show, we'll turn back to check on her," I said.

The boom of a gun blast shattered the night. It was close, the sound pounding our ears. An eruption of water shot up twenty yards in front of our small flotilla. We were being shot at!

"Hey, there are people down here in the water. Stop shooting!" I yelled.

I waved my kayakers toward the bank.

"Stay low and hug the shore."

"Where are you going, Emma?" Sofia asked.

"I'll be right back." I brushed aside my cotton button-up shirt and reached into the belly-band holster. The cold steel of the handgun brought a sense of comfort.

My paddle sounded as soft as the gentle waves lapping on the bank. I pulled the kayak through the water toward the gunshot. The inlet there was shallow and murky. Cattails and phragmites reeds were thick around its opening, and the heavy fog cast a pallor over the pristine waterway. The air smelled of rotting leaves and swamp mud.

I pulled the kayak into the bank and stepped into the oozing mud near shore.

Another shot sounded and slapped the water a few yards from where I stood. I gripped my semi-auto 9mm, pointed it at the clouds and touched off the trigger. Boom!

"Emma!" Sofia yelled behind me.

"Who are you?" I yelled. "I'm armed. Come out."

I heard a rustling in the reeds and stepped fully into the opening. A shadowy figure raced away through the thick, foggy marsh. The rapid sloshing footfalls indicated at least two sets of feet. I could make out the white jacket the one closest to me wore as their steps carried them deeper into the heavy mist.

"Stop," I yelled and shot into the air again, but their progress continued. They knew or were willing to take the chance that I wouldn't shoot them.

I tried to give chase for a moment, but the swamp mud and my water shoes did not cooperate . After digging my footwear out of the mire twice, I conceded defeat. The shooter or shooters were out of sight and long gone by then, anyway.

"It's safe now, ladies," I said.

"Are you sure?"

"Safer here than there," I said. "The shooter was running away close to the shore in your general direction. He's likely headed to one of the houses on Beacon Hill."

I heard their paddles hit the water as soon as I spoke. Their paddling skills had improved dramatically since we started. Their kayaks pulled up even with mine in seconds.

I slipped my phone from its waterproof bag and dialed Sam's number.

"Emma, is everything okay?"

"It's been better, Sam. Someone was shooting near us. Their shots struck the water just a few yards in front of us. I shot back, up in the air, of course, and they ran off."

"Did you see who it was? Could they still be in the area?"

"No, and no. At least, I think not. I saw them well enough to see they were hot-footing away from us."

I looked back toward home and saw a small light on the water.

"Katrina is coming this way," I said, and the younger women looked up.

"Thank God, she's okay," Sofia said.

"Where was Katrina? Did you get separated during the shooting?"

"She just needed a potty break, Sam. It's okay, deep breaths…"

"Are you coming back now? No, never mind, wait right where you are. I'm coming to get the three of you in the sheriff's department's skiff. What's your position?"

"We're at the small inlet just before that big housing development, River's End," I said.

"Of course—where the murder was last year. Comforting to know."

"We're fine, Sam. We can paddle back, can't we, ladies?" I asked loud enough for them to hear.

"I'm good with being picked up," Sofia said.

"Me too," Val said.

"I guess I'm outvoted. Not a good indicator for

future repeat business."

"What in the world happened up here? Were those gunshots I heard?" Katrina asked as soon as she was close enough for us to hear.

"There was someone in the swamp shooting at us. I thought they were going to kill us. Emma shot back at them, and they ran off," Sofia explained.

"Let's get out of here then. What are we waiting for, Emma?"

I held up one finger, asking her to wait a moment, but she turned her kayak around and started paddling.

"Come on, Sofia. Let's go," Katrina said.

"Is that Katrina?" Sam asked. "Is she back?"

"Yes, and she's being her usual stubborn self, Sam." I shifted in my seat. "Katrina, please wait. Sam is coming out for us," I said. "I'll bet some kids snuck out with their daddy's hunting rifle and were shooting up beer cans."

"Is that really what you think?" Sam asked in my ear.

"Not one hundred percent, but it works for now."

"I see. Okay, I'm in the skiff now, and the motor is running. I'll be there in two shakes."

"Sounds good. See you then." The fog lifted for a moment, blowing away in sheets of cotton. Finally, a good sign, I thought.

"Oh, my God!" The scream tore across the water. It was a primordial screech, full of terror and pain. The sound of a rabbit caught in the fox's jaws or a mother who lost her child. The very sound sent shivers down my back. I pointed my flashlight's beam at the source.

"What's going on? Emma, are you there? What's happening?" Sam asked.

The flashlight beam settled on Val's face, slack-jawed and paler than the full moon. She looked at me with wild eyes and pointed at the bank. I directed my light there.

"Sam, there's a dead body shoved into the cattails. You better call it in."

Chapter Two

By the time Katrina and Sofia paddled back to where Val and I waited, Sam was there. I'd inspected the body but didn't touch or disturb it in any way, not without gloves. The victim was female and, by my guesstimate, in her early twenties. It was impossible for me to tell how long the body had been there. The water had saturated the woman's skin, but she didn't look familiar. I found that surprising in a town as small as ours.

The conversation stalled after the three of us climbed into the skiff. Val's hands were shaking. Sofia stared blankly toward the shore. Katrina seemed the most composed, but she'd missed most of the excitement. Sam kept trying to lighten their mood and would mix in an occasional "cop question." He'd get a response if the question required only a yes or no answer. If more was needed, the women gazed off into the distance and shrugged. Shocked, I guess.

When the lights from two Boston Whaler skiffs lit up the night and headed in our direction, their tongues loosened, and they began to calm down. The Sheriff's Department arrived soon after, and I mean the whole Sheriff's Office. Our esteemed Sheriff John Wathen himself had crawled out of bed to attend. It was his first late-night duty since the Policeman's Ball. Everyone always feels safer in numbers—even when there is no safety. One of my criminal justice instructors was ex-military. Whenever we gathered in a group, he'd remind us that one grenade or a single sniper would take us all out at once. He carried shrapnel in his chest to prove it. Others who were with him that fateful day weren't as lucky.

"I can't believe you ran into that swamp with someone firing a gun, Emma," Katrina said. "What were you thinking?"

"We were being shot at. I couldn't see the shooter and didn't know his intentions. I thought it was the only way to ensure our safety. That's my job on the water, Kat."

"I guess they teach you lots of stuff like that with your training. I'm glad you were there, Emma. It could've turned out worse."

"It was bad enough, Kat…" I said.

"I couldn't carry a gun;" Val said. "I don't even like looking at them. They scare me."

"I don't think about it. It's just a tool of the trade."

"Could you shoot someone, Emma?" Val asked. "I couldn't, but I hate to kill anything."

"She's telling the truth there," Sofia said. "I remember in high school the fit she gave our biology teacher about how awful it was to kill frogs to dissect."

"I'll bet you eat crabs, though. Huh, Val?" I asked.

"Well, I am from St. Miriam's County, right? A girl must draw the line somewhere."

"I think there's a law or something about that, isn't there, Deputy Sam?" Kat asked.

"Indeed, I'd have to run you in for violating Title 10: Crimes against Public Health, Conduct, and Sensitivities. In this scenario, there might be a follow-up charge under Title 11 for Indecency and Obscenity." Sam smiled, and all three of my kayaking ladies laughed.

It was good to see the women coming around and being able to joke a bit.

"Did you have any good P.I. cases over the winter, Emma?" Sofia asked.

"Let me forewarn you, Emma," Katrina said. "My sister thinks she's interested in a criminal justice degree and that what you do is exciting. Hopefully, tonight will put her in a different frame of mind."

"Oh no. I don't think I could handle field work, Katrina. I'm hoping for something a bit more sedate."

"You've got plenty of 'sedate' already in the bakery with me, Sofia."

"Do you think? After the bakery break-in, I wonder if anywhere is all that safe. Maybe I could get a desk job doing research for the police or a P.I. assistant. That I think I could handle."

"I can only comment on investigating. It has its ups and downs. I spend a lot of time sitting on my backside, waiting for something to happen. Too often, you learn things about your friends and neighbors that you'd rather not know. That can be messy, especially in a small town like ours," I said.

"Stick with baking, Sofia. It's safer, steadier, and has no dead people. Plus, I'd miss you. By the way, are there any updates on my vandals, Sam?" Katrina asked.

"Not much to report," Sam said. "We dusted for prints, as you know; sorry about all the powder on everything. We're still waiting for print matches from the lab, although I imagine there will be a lot of prints from your customers. It won't be easy to thin them out and narrow the search. Were you able to complete the inventory? Besides the money, was there anything else missing?"

"As far as we've determined, that was it."

The sheriff's boat moved toward us, its motor idling. When it pulled alongside. John Wathen threw the bow rope to Sam.

"Do you think there's any sense in trying to get the hounds back here, Major? You know more about them than I do."

"I can contact Mr. Russell if you like, Sheriff, but I think I know his answer. It's too wet to hold the perp's scent, not to mention the smell of the swamp gas fouling their noses. I doubt the dogs could follow a track in there."

"I thought the same thing." The sheriff waved his hands at the other boat, and three deputies jumped into the murky water.

"Did you have any questions for the women tonight, Sheriff?" Sam asked. "I want to get them back home if not."

"No, we've held them up long enough tonight. I'd appreciate it if all of you would stop by the office tomorrow to give us a statement. Will you be able to do that?"

"Yes, sir," they answered in unison.

As Sam turned the boat away, I turned back toward the men in the water. They were pulling the body out of the reeds. I guessed that was why Sam was hurrying to leave, so my clients didn't have to see that. And they'd already seen enough. Tonight's events would be the main feature in their nightmares for the foreseeable future.

****

The boat ride home was smooth and uneventful.

As I tied us up to the dock, Sofia and Val thanked me for an adventure they wouldn't soon forget.

"Forget?" Katrina asked. "I think it will be one story you'll still be telling when you have grandchildren to listen to it. They'll probably be the only ones in the state who haven't heard it by then, anyway."

"We'd rather you keep the details of this evening to yourselves, at least for the time being, ladies. It might help us to catch the killer."

"Hey, no problem, Sam," Valerie said. "I hope that degenerate murderer doesn't know who I am at all. I'll be happy when he's behind bars."

"You are treating this as a murder, then, Sam?" I asked.

He gave a subtle shake of his head. Nothing more would be said in our mixed company.

When Kat climbed out of the boat, something metallic clunked against its side. There was no splash; I assumed she had carried something heavy in her purse.

"Why doesn't everyone stop by the bakery in the morning?" she asked. "I have some awesome black raspberry-filled donuts. The filling is from a new supplier and is as good as fresh from the vines."

"Maybe after donuts and coffee, we can go to the sheriff's office together? Do you think that would be okay, Sam?" Sofia asked.

"That would be fine, although we'll need to take individual statements from each of you."

We said our goodbyes at the water's edge. All three thanked me for an interesting night afloat and said they'd plan to do it again soon. I doubted their sincerity.

If they ever paddled another kayak, I'd be surprised, but for sure, it wouldn't be a moonlight excursion.

Sam helped me untie the kayaks we'd towed home. We stowed them in the racks and watched Katrina's SUV's taillights disappear down our driveway.

"That wasn't a good start—not for the night tours anyway," Sam said.

"No, I might have to reevaluate. Maybe it wasn't the best idea, the whole night thing. I thought it would be something different that nobody else offered. I'm sure the news about the inaugural float will be all over town by the morning."

"Did you have any impressions from the crime scene? How long was Katrina gone from the group?"

"No, Sam. Please don't try to draw me into this case." I said.

"After how you handled the situation tonight, I thought you were over everything, past the anxieties from last year. The town needs a private detective, and the sheriff's office can still use a consultant."

"Do you think I'm afraid? You think that's why I don't want in on any cases?"

"You're fearless, Emma, though nobody could blame you if you were afraid. You were in death's doorway on more than one occasion last fall. You're a natural at investigating, and most folks enjoy the things they do well."

"I'm not afraid, Sam. I'm tired of it. I've been exposing people's soiled laundry the entire winter and ruined families. I've left children without both of their parents. I need some distance from the bowels of society."

"Is that why you refused to chime in on the River's

End murder minutes after you found your sister-in-law and brought her home safe?"

"All the while destroying a family I'd known all my life."

"And who deserved it."

"Not all of them."

"Please understand me, Emma. I'm all for whatever makes you happy, or if not doing something does. I don't want to twist your arm to do anything. I am just worried about you. Artists must paint. Writers must write…"

"And you? Is that what you've always wanted to do? What you *must* do—give out speeding tickets and harass teenage boys?"

Sam's face fell, and his eyes dropped.

"Is that what you think about what I do?" he asked. "I feel I'm protecting our community, keeping the roads we drive on safe and keeping our neighbors secure in their homes at night."

"I'm sorry, Sam. No, that's not what I think, and you're right. I guess I don't know what I want."

"Do you want to talk about it, Em?"

I smiled and touched his cheek. "Don't get me wrong, Sam. I do enjoy the chase. But I had illusions of what being an investigator would be, but this winter was one of disillusionment. I wanted to help people and the chance to catch the bad guy. Maybe it was all pride—the knight in shining armor syndrome, protecting the innocent, and all that. A goal more appropriate for a teenage boy hoping to impress his teenage princess crush than a thirty-something me."

"You want to help people, Em. You always have, and that's a noble thing."

"Maybe, and maybe it was just hubris, and it took a season of catching cheaters for it to sink in. This winter, it was all about infidelity, Mrs. Abell's missing cat, and one case of a rural mailbox mutilation."

"I bet Mrs. Abell loved you for finding her tabby."

"Humpf, except I never did, Sam. I'm still looking for Misty. My favorite case in the last three months was the lady who thought her husband was stepping out with another woman. Turns out he was. She was a party planner helping him with the details for their surprise tenth-anniversary party. Of course, I couldn't tell her until after the party, and I didn't get paid, but it did bring some satisfaction."

"The big cases, the important ones, don't pop up every day, not in small-town Newtowne, and that's a good thing," Sam said.

"I know, and you are right, but I need time to ground myself. It gets so dirty, and if you play with the pigs, some of the slop rubs off on you."

"Not on you, Emma. Regarding decency, you're the Teflon woman; none of the slop sticks."

"No, plenty stuck to me. I caught two cheating husbands and one wife. Two couples had children; the third couple wasn't much more than newlyweds. They'll always remember me as the one who ruined their lives. Even their kids will grow up to hate me."

"They'll remember the spouse who betrayed them and the parent who didn't love and honor their family. You were the Light-Bringer and shined your flashlight on their dirty little secret. Because of you, they won't live a lie and waste their love on the undeserving."

"You do know that Light-Bringer is one of the names for Lucifer, the devil, don't you?"

"Um, no…well, no…you're not that, not at all. You're the flashlight beam controller person…like that Greek guy. You're a fighter for truth, justice, and the American way."

"Have I heard that somewhere before? So, am I more Diogenes or superhero? Do I need to find a cape?"

"Besides all your wonderful traits, I love you, too. What more could any woman ask for?"

He smiled in his big, goofy way, hugged me, and kissed the top of my head. It was hard to stay perturbed at my big clown of a boyfriend for very long.

"I love you, too, Deputy. But I'm still not getting involved."

"Maybe I could bounce an idea or two off you for a second opinion?"

"Okay, but I'm not doing any detective work. Besides, you've got people for that."

"So, are you in for donuts and coffee at the bakery in the morning?" Sam asked.

"Yes, that sounds good. I want to make sure Kat, Sofia, and Val are doing okay after what we went through. I also have a beginner kayak class, so I can't dawdle long."

"And you, Emma? How are you doing, Sweetheart?"

"I'm fine." I paused in thought for a moment. "I don't think your victim was shot, Sam, or at least not killed by the shooter tonight. The body looked like it was in the water for a while, so why was the gunman there?"

"Maybe he was trying to scare you off until he could permanently dispose of the body?"

"Is an autopsy always done in cases like this?"

"Yes, why?"

"They might have tried to confuse the cause of death for some reason," I said.

"There's still the possibility, however slight, that the shooter had nothing to do with the crime. How close was he to the victim when you spotted him running?"

"I'd say twenty-five yards, give or take, and I can't even say for sure that it was a 'he'."

"Is it possible he or she didn't even know the body was there? As you said, it could have been a kid taking potshots at the water."

"Maybe, but that's a bit of a stretch, don't you think?" I asked.

Sam tugged at the edges of his newly sprouted mustache. A nervous habit he'd picked up along with the facial hair when he was deep in thought.

"Well, after we give our statements tomorrow," I said, "I want to forget the whole thing. I'm sure tonight's kayakers will feel the same way. After that, I have the kayaking lesson and the rest of the day in the garden."

"You want to meet for an early lunch before the kayak lessons? You'd be home in plenty of time and still can get your gardening in."

"Maybe a quick burger at the Pub? I love their fries with the seafood seasoning."

"It's a date," Sam said.

Sleep didn't come easy that night. The images of the deceased woman flashed repeatedly in my mind. I'd had too much darkness in my life in the past few months and had a bad feeling about this case. I couldn't allow my desire to know to overwhelm my need for peace.

Sam switched off the nightstand light. It was decorated with shells I'd collected from the beach, a project I'd done with our long-time family friend Abby's help when I was young. It was intended to be a gift for my parents. A gift that they never received.

Abby was in an asylum now, in large part because of me. She'd murdered her husband, kidnapped my sister-in-law, and played a role in my sister's death as well. She was where she deserved and needed to be. Even knowing that was still hard. I hated her. I hated what she'd done, and I'd helped convict her. Someone who was almost a mother to me once—in what seemed a different life. Where did it all go wrong?

Chapter Three

Katrina didn't lie. Jelly-filled donuts weren't my normal breakfast fare when I had time to eat healthier, but whatever concoction she'd stuffed into the sweet treats was inspired. At the first bite, my eyes flew open. I could have cried. They were that good. It was what heaven must taste like, and I wondered what sorcerer's trick had captured it for mere mortals' pleasure.

"Oh…Oh my, these are just too good," Val said. "Can I get a few to take home with me? Kiss my diet goodbye for this week."

"Like you need to be on a diet. But of course, you can," Katrina said. "How about a dozen?"

"There's just me, you know, Katrina? There's no Mister Valerie and a house full of rugrats waiting for me at home, but maybe a half dozen?"

Sofia laughed and choked on a half-swallowed bite. She held a napkin to her mouth and coughed. Her face turned red, and her eyes watered.

I slapped her on the back between the shoulder blades, and after a moment, she recovered enough to speak.

"Okay, guys, be serious here now. You've made me waste half of my donut."

"I guess you'll have to eat another one then," Val said. "It wouldn't do for me to be the only fat ex-cheerleader at our high school reunion."

"By the way, Emma, where's Sam?"

"He begged off, so the interrogation room can be ready for us. That will be a regrettable decision when we tell him about these donuts."

"Interrogation room? That sounds ominous." Val wiped the jelly remnants from her lacquered nails. She then rubbed off her red lipstick and inspected her lips in a compact mirror she pulled from her purse. She separated her black hair into two sections and tied them back into pigtails.

"What are you doing, Val?" Sofia asked.

"Hey, if I'm going to be interrogated by a bunch of small-town cops, I will do my best little girl impersonation."

"Let's go with the interview room then. I think that's what they're calling it now, anyway."

"A rose by any other name?" Sofia joked.

"I think Sam will take our statements unless he's been called away, so you have nothing to worry about."

"Speaking of no-shows, I wonder where Pastor Frank is today? He comes in every morning around this time."

"And he always gets these same donuts, too," Sofia said. "I guess they've been given the Heavenly Quality Award."

"What is in these things, Kat?" I asked. "It's kind of like Blackberry, but it's different. It has a slight twang."

"It's a secret family recipe. I have a new supplier for the jelly, and he doesn't use any fillers. Of course, I add my little something-something, but I'm not telling you about that."

"Well, I'm guessing a more thorough interrogation

won't loosen your lips about the donuts, so we might as well make our way to the sheriff's department," I said. "Ready, ladies?"

"Sure, let's get it over with." Val flipped her pigtails and gave us a big, innocent smile.

****

Sam met us as we reached the front door of the station.

"Come on in, ladies. Can I offer you a cup of coffee?"

"I'd advise against it," I said. "Unless your taste buds lean toward day-old mud."

"I think we'll pass," Sofia said.

We were separated into two groups. Sam would take Val and Katrina's statements, and Deputy Joyce would interview Sofia and me.

Sofia went in first and was back out in about ten minutes.

"I see you survived, but you do look a bit pale. Are you okay?" I asked.

"Sure, I'm good. That was just a first for me. Hospitals and police stations both give me the heebie-jeebies."

Deputy Joyce opened the door then and gestured me inside.

"How have you been, Deputy?"

"It's still just Joyce, Emma." She held up one finger and flipped on the recorder on the table between us.

"Please state your full name for the official record."

"Emma Louise Love."

"Miss Love, I need you to tell me in your own

words what transpired last night. You'll be recorded, of course. You're not a suspect currently, but if you want a lawyer at any time, please tell me." Joyce reached out and flipped the off button.

"Sorry. Now that we have that out of the way, how have you been, Emma? Is the major treating you right, or do I need to straighten him out?"

"We're good, Joyce, but I may call on you sometime to do just that." I smiled.

"Are you ready to give your statement?"

I nodded, and she flipped it on to record.

"There isn't much to tell, as I'm sure Sofia already reported."

"Yes, ma'am. But in your words, please…"

"Okay, it was my first night outing with clients; I called it a Moonlight Tour. Four women signed up for the inaugural float, but one didn't show. That left Katrina Baker, her sister Sofia, and Sofia's friend, Valerie. I don't know her last name."

"It's Valerie Simmons."

"Simmons, okay. Anyway, the four of us launched our kayaks around nine p.m. We intended to paddle to the mouth of the bay past the River's End subdivision, then double back along the opposite shore. We were almost at the end of the first leg when we heard a shot that landed in the water in front of us. I yelled to advise the shooter that we were in the line of fire, then asked the ladies to hug the bank with their kayaks."

"All three of them?"

"No, Katrina had lagged behind for a nature call."

"Go ahead."

"I eased my kayak into the inlet there and unholstered my pistol. I have a concealed-weapons permit. That's when the shooter fired again, missing me by a couple of feet. I shot into the air to make him aware that I was armed. I caught sight of him retreating into the marsh, but the fog was too thick to allow me to see any identifying features."

"You gave chase, I understand?"

"I tried, but the marsh mud was as good as a rope tied around my ankles. I didn't go more than a few steps."

Joyce opened her notepad. "How did the perp manage to run then?"

"Boots, I guess? Or the ground was higher and drier where they were."

"How long was Katrina Baker separated from your party?"

"I'd guess maybe fifteen minutes. In stressful situations, though, time can play tricks on a person."

"In your opinion, do you think Miss Baker had time to get to the spot on the bank where the shooting occurred and then return to her original position?"

"I can't say for sure, but Kat wouldn't. It all happened fast."

"Then what happened?"

"I phoned Sam—Major Mattingley, and told him about being shot at. He offered to come get us in the skiff, and the ladies in my group wanted to take him up on the offer. Before we disconnected, Valerie screamed and pointed at the body in the cattails. Sam called in the reinforcements. He got there a bit before they did, and we climbed in the skiff and tied the kayaks on to tow behind us. The rest, you know."

Joyce glanced at her notepad again. "Was there any attempt by your clients to compare stories or challenge what you'd seen?"

"No, of course not, Joyce."

"Did any of your group touch or attempt to move the body?" she asked.

"You know I know better than that, but the body looked like it was in the water for a while."

"Did any of you remove anything from the scene?" Joyce asked.

"Really? None of us had anything to do with it. Okay? Is John Wathen trying to hang this on us? Is this about me getting the goods on his brother…?"

Joyce flipped the recorder off.

"I'm sorry, Emma. The questions were his idea—at his insistence, I might add. And yes, it probably is because of Robert's sentence. Watch yourself around him. He has a mean streak, and he holds grudges."

"Thanks, I'm aware. I've known his family for a long time."

****

I left Joyce in a less-than-happy mood and met Sam as he exited the second interview room.

"All done?" he asked.

"Yes. When are you running for Sheriff so we can kick this vindictive moron out of office?"

Sam held one finger to his lips.

"Maybe next election. I've wanted to talk to you about it, but what's happening?"

"Nothing, just Joyce putting me through the third degree after being told to by your sheriff. Same old thing. What about that lunch you promised me? I brought you a donut from Katrina's for dessert."

"Newtowne Pub?"

"Yes, please."

As we both had plans after lunch, Sam took his patrol car, and I drove my trusty old Bronco. It's trusty, not rusty, although some confuse the two.

We ordered our burgers. Sam ordered a bacon cheeseburger, and I got a mushroom and Swiss burger, both with well-seasoned fries, of course.

"What did you get from the ladies you interviewed? Anything we didn't already know."

"No, it was a dead end, but we must dot our i's and cross our t's." Sam dropped his eyes to the dessert menu, then back up at me, not to my eyes but to the part in my hair. I thought for a moment that I must have a zit. It's been a while since Sam tried to lie to me.

"You see that guy over there, the one in the green plaid flannel shirt? He's in a relationship with the woman sitting across from him, wife, girlfriend, mistress—I don't know. She's mad, and he's lying to her about whatever she's mad about. He won't look her in the eyes; his eyes are everywhere. He gave you a good stare when we walked in. Guess he thought you might be policing his indiscretions as the morality police. He can't sit still, and a moment ago, I read his lips when he answered a heated question. He said no while nodding his head yes."

"I know you're good at this, Emma. Are we playing our game?"

"No, but the point is that I don't know that guy, and I can see he's lying. I do know you, and you're not very good at it. So, try again, Sam. What did Kat or Val say that we didn't already know?"

"Sorry, Em, I don't want to lie to you. I'm trying not to drag you into this, and it wasn't much. Katrina said she was off on her nature break for so long because she'd taken up smoking again and didn't want anyone to know. She claimed she did her call of nature thing, then got her fix of menthol, nicotine, and tar."

"Claimed she did?"

"She had a new pack. She even showed it to me. It was in a fancy metal case, but not even one was missing. She had trouble figuring out the latch to open it with, and she didn't smell like cigarettes. I got close enough to tell. I took a sniff of her hair and asked what shampoo she used. I told her it smelled good, and you might want to try it."

"She probably thought you were flirting with her, Sam. She'll be hand-delivering your donuts to your office from now on."

"You don't have to worry, Emma. She's no competition."

"Who said I was worried?"

"Why don't you let me try that donut you've bragged about? You never know; that might change my mind."

"I guess I'll take my chances. Anyone can buy them at the bakery. No association or relationship with the baker is required. Was there anything else?"

"That's it, scout's honor."

"Well, you enjoy your donut, Sam. I must hit the road if I'm going to get any gardening in before the kids show up."

"Kids?"

"Four teenagers, two boys and two girls, are taking the kayak lesson at three o'clock. I guess it's after they get off school."

"Have the boys help you tote the kayaks down to the water. It will give them a chance to impress their girlfriends."

"See you at home, Sam, and quit sniffing women's hair. It's unbecoming."

****

The bad part about starting a garden on new ground is the established weeds. Having their roots in the same ground for so long, they don't want to give up. Despite weed killer, landscaping fabric, and a good old-fashioned beat-down with my hoe, they didn't catch on to the inevitable. They never would, but this was my vegetable patch now.

Some might say the weedy persistence was admirable, well, non-gardeners perhaps. As a gardener, I knew their effort was futile. It was a waste of time and energy sticking with what they'd known, casting their seeds, and spreading their roots in unwelcoming soil. I would overcome their efforts. They reminded me of folks who get in a rut or are hesitant to try something new. People tend to stick with the known and familiar. The status quo is king, and weeds are as stubborn as we are.

Young Josh "Crab" Grimes had borrowed his father's rotary tiller and worked the soil for me as soon as the ground was dry enough that it wouldn't clump. He wasn't a large lad and had to fight the tiller, or it would carry him off, but he was as determined as the weeds.

With my hoe in hand, I attacked the sprouting lamb's-quarter, crabgrass, and plantain. There was a small patch of purslane growing wild in one corner. I'd let it go for its nutty flavor in salads. There beginning sprouts of wild asparagus near the kayak launch as well. I love my cultivated veggies, but I never turn my nose up at volunteers, either.

Often, I lose track of time when I'm in the garden. My four adventurous teens pulled into my driveway as I carried my hoe back to the garden shed. I stashed it on my way to greet them. They looked prepared as they stepped out of the 1980s vintage Ford. Each carried a bag, a water bottle, and a life preserver vest.

"Hello, everyone. I'm Emma Love. Welcome to Love's Kayaking Floats and Tours."

"Hi, Mrs. Love, I'm Roxy. I'm pleased to meet you." She was a short, thin girl with jet-black hair shaved on the sides in a fade and a ghost's head pendant hanging from a chain around her neck. Her skin was as pale as moonlight in contrast to her black lipstick and fingernails. I reminded myself to grab sunscreen for everyone.

"It's Miss, and Emma is fine, Roxy. Pleased to meet you also. And who's your sturdy-looking young man?"

The four of them laughed.

"Oh, he's not mine…well, I mean, he's my brother, Martin."

Crew-cut, freckled, and sunburned, Martin held out his hand and shook mine. He looked more like a weathered Marine than a teenager. He was a weightlifter, for sure, hopefully without the benefit of steroids. I wondered how the two of them could have sprouted from the same family unit.

"I've seen you on the water in your kayak, Emma. It looks like fun. I work part-time with my dad on his fishing boat."

"Marty is with me," a slightly heavy-set girl said. "I'm Savannah. Savannah Olsen. My father's the mayor." She flipped back her blonde curls and grabbed Marty's hand in hers. She didn't offer her hand until I stuck mine out, then smiled as her fingers closed around my hand.

I turned to the remaining boy. "Jerome Somerville," he said as we shook hands. "I'm with Roxanne. I think you know my oldest sister, ma'am. She's the head nurse on the third floor, Nurse Jackie? She thought you might remember her and said to tell you hello."

"I sure do. Jackie is a force of nature, as I'm sure you know. I've been intending to give her a call. She was a comfort to me when I needed just that. Personal question, Jerome?"

"Sure. I guess."

"Did the bat symbol carved in your hair come about before or after you started dating Roxy?"

The teens all laughed, and Martin slapped Jerome on the back.

"Before, but it might've helped me to convince her to go out with me." Jerome smiled.

"Okay, guys. Now that we know each other, we'll be ready to go as soon as I grab the kayaks. Are there any questions so far?"

"I'll have plenty when we hit the water," Roxy said.

"Maybe you young men would like to give me a hand?" I asked.

"We'll get the kayaks for you, Emma," Martin said, pulling Jerome toward the rack.

I smiled and thought of Sam's remark. "What gentlemen you are," I said, both in appreciation and in the hope of garnering them some extra "boyfriend points."

"Any particular ones, Emma?" Jerome asked.

"The five of them on the grass that I pulled off the rack already."

I was feeling good about the day and this group of young people. They were from sharply divergent economic groups and different school cliques. Despite their contrasts, they were together as friends, exploring something new, which gave me hope for the world.

"Can I ask you a personal question, Emma?" Roxy asked.

"Sure, what's sauce for the goose and all that..."

"Huh?"

"Never mind. What did you want to ask me?"

"What was it like finding a dead body?"

"Boy, news travels fast around here."

"Small town, Newtowne," Jerome said as he set the first kayak at the water's edge.

"I wouldn't recommend putting it on your bucket list, Roxy. It's gross and scary, and I hope it never happens again."

"That might not be easy in your line of work," Savannah said. "How does your live-in boyfriend feel about your working a man's job?"

I bit my lip before answering, and then Roxy did so for me.

"Wow, Savannah, 1960 called and wants its misogyny back," Roxy said. "Don't let any man limit you from doing what you want. Not my brother and not your daddy either."

I liked her immediately.

I gave my usual spiel about boat safety, a rundown of paddle strokes, and advised them to point the kayak into any waves stirred up by powerboats.

The trip was a dream. The teenagers got along great, and except for a few references to dead bodies, it was also peaceful. I didn't know it would be my last hours of peace for a while. As we neared the dock, Jerome paddled to my side.

"I wanted to tell you something, but Jackie said not to let anyone else hear."

"What is it, Jerome?"

"She has information about the woman you found last night. She wants you to come see her."

"She needs to call the sheriff, Jerome."

"She doesn't trust anyone there except maybe your boyfriend."

"I can't. I'm trying to stay out of police business."

"Okay, I'll tell her."

"No, never mind, don't do that," I said. "Jackie is a friend. I'll go see her after we get back."

Chapter Four

The boys helped load the kayaks on the rack, and they all assured me they'd had an incredible adventure and would return with more friends. They promised to text me the pictures they'd taken of a mother otter and her babies playing on the riverbank. They'd repeatedly slid down the bank, then climbed back up to do it again. Martin thought he had a decent video of their play as well.

I quickly showered, and my cell rang as I was drying off.

"How did the float go, Emma?"

"It was great, Sam. How's the detecting? Have you identified the woman yet?"

"No, she's not a local for sure. We have a sketch of her going out on the wire tonight to see if we can get any hits."

"I might have something later."

"How's that?"

"One of my kayakers today was Jerome Somerville. He's Nurse Jackie's little brother, remember her?"

"I'm not likely to forget. If I recall correctly, we voted her 'most desirable companion in a street fight' last year."

"That's Jackie. Jerome says she knows something about the woman and wants to talk to me."

"Look, Emma, I know you didn't want to get pulled in on this case. Tell him to have her call me or stop by the station."

"He says Jackie only trusts me and *maybe* you, his words, so you're welcome to meet me there if you're free."

"I would, but I have a dried flower to take to the university botanist. We found a white flower with yellow stamens in the victim's pocket. No idea if it's a clue or not, but it's worth checking into. Are you comfortable going alone?"

"With Jackie? Of course. Is there anything else I should know?"

"Well, as you asked, we did get word back from the coroner on the time of death. She estimates it was twenty to twenty-four hours before the discovery of the body. She doesn't have a cause of death yet, but there were no bullet wounds. So, we're not sure what to make of your shooter."

"There's a chance it was just some kid then," I said.

"Maybe, but one other thing, Emma. I'm not sure if I should mention it…"

"Well, you've started now, so you have to."

"Cheryl Pratt, isn't she your cousin?"

"She is, but maybe you remember her as Cheryl Love? She married Preacher Frank from the Bay View Church. Dad's brother Gene is her father. Why? Is Cheryl in trouble?"

"No, but she came to see me today. Frank hasn't been home since they had lunch together yesterday afternoon, and she's worried."

"I'm sure she is. Maybe I'll give her a call when I

get back from the hospital, but Frank's probably home by now. Cheryl is such a worrywart.. What did you tell her?"

"Not much. I wrote it up. She said he'd done it in the past, but not for many years, since college, in fact. I guess he had a drinking problem before he found religion. A case where God saved a soul in the here and now from the sound of it."

"Okay, I'll let you know what Jackie has to say. Drive safely."

****

I asked for Jackie at the third-floor nurse's station. The candy striper in front of the computer said she was on her rounds and would return in a moment. I turned away from the desk, and there she stood.

"Are you looking for me, Emma?"

"I sure am. How have you been, Jackie?" I stepped toward her, and we hugged.

"It's been a while," Jackie said. "Are you bringing trouble to town again?"

"Oh no. I don't bring it, but it does seem to find me no matter how well I hide."

"I guess that's why you're here?"

"Yeah. I met that handsome young brother of yours today. Jerome seems like a nice kid. He told me that—"

"Let's walk down to the break room, Emma. We can talk there."

We went down the hall and through two sets of doors to one marked "Employees Only." When Jackie held it open for me, I felt like I'd been admitted to a secret inner sanctum forbidden to the uninitiated.

Two older nurses sat drinking sodas and chatting about an elderly patient's treatment protocols. They stopped their chat and stared at us.

"Do we have a problem, ladies?" Jackie asked. Their eyes turned back to each other.

We sat at the farthest table away from the two of them.

"Sorry I had to drag you out here, Emma, but I don't get a warm fuzzy from John Wathen's crew at the sheriff's department. No offense to your Sam."

"Jerome said you might know something about the Jane Doe found in the bay?"

"Yes, but only because I happened to drop by the morgue this morning before the body was sent to the coroner in Baltimore. I knew I'd seen the woman before. It took me a while to remember, but then it came to me. Aren't you and Katrina Baker friends?"

"I guess. Old acquaintances, anyway. Why?"

"I was across the street from the bus stop when I saw that woman. She got off the bus with another woman, and they seemed chummy. The other woman had long, straight black hair. They came out together and got in a car that Sofia Baker was driving."

"Are you sure it was Sofia driving?"

"It's hard to mistake Sofia with her new rainbow hairdo, plus I know her car. We shared a fender bender in the hospital parking lot a couple of months back."

"I'm surprised Sofia never mentioned anything about the accident. She was in the group I had out kayaking when the body was found. Then again, they only saw a leg and a muddy shoe from where they were."

"I wouldn't put too much stock in it, but I thought you and Sam should know. I guess you see the dregs of humanity doing what you do for a living."

"That's why I need a break from it, Jackie. You get to thinking the worst things about people."

"Not me, I hope." Jackie laughed. "I'm sure it was perfectly innocent, Emma."

"I know, and as I said, none of them saw the woman up close. I hope the woman wasn't their friend who missed out on kayaking. They said she'd been out of touch."

"There ya go. Well, girl, I must get back to work. It's been a slow night so far, but that's apt to change at any moment. You either work your butt off, or you sit on it around here…there's no in-between. Give me a call sometime and we'll get together."

"Thanks, Jackie. I'd love that, and thanks for the information, too. I'll pass it along to Sam."

I considered what Jackie had told me on the elevator ride to the hospital lobby. Were Sofia, Valerie, and the unknown woman involved in a lover's quarrel that ended up deadly? Val must have been familiar enough with the dead woman to share a bus trip with her. Sofia also to have picked her up at the bus stop.

When the elevator doors opened, my phone rang. The number looked familiar and was local, but it wasn't set up in my contacts.

"Hello?"

"Emma, this is Cheryl Love Pratt. Remember me, cousin?"

"Of course I do, Cheryl. I heard you retired from teaching and opened a local florist shop. How is your family doing?

"It's been a while, Emmy. My family? Well, I'm okay, and I guess I'm the only member of my immediate family at the moment."

"I know you went through a lot, Cheryl…"

"Yes, there were some rough years after Dad passed, as you can imagine. Even before then, after Mom went. They were teenage sweethearts, you know, my mom and dad? But that isn't why I called, I…"

"I didn't know, Cheryl, but can I call you back? I'd love to catch up, but…"

"You didn't hear?"

"Hear what, Cheryl? Is this about Frank?"

"Yes, He's still missing, Emma. So, Sam did mention it to you?"

"Sam said Frank didn't come home last night. I thought he'd be back by now, though. Is there still no word from him?"

"Nothing. He took his car so he could be anywhere—in a ditch or off with some woman. I'm hoping you'll do me a big favor, Emma?"

"I will if I can, Cheryl."

"I believe Frank has been seeing someone else. I didn't want to say anything to Sam because I wouldn't want it to be in the public record, not with Frank's standing in the community and all."

"Yes, I can see that being an issue for a pastor. Why do you think he's been unfaithful?"

"Frank says he's counseling someone. There are late-night phone calls and running off to the church at all hours. One night, I parked outside his church, and a young woman came out with him. I couldn't make out who she was. Frank got in the car with her and talked for ten minutes or more. When she got out and started her car, I left, but it was another hour before Frank came home."

"Sam mentioned he once had a drinking problem

and might've fallen off the wagon. I know that's bad enough, but maybe that's all there is to it, Cheryl. I'm sure he's counseled parishioners in the past. It's his job, isn't it?"

"He's never been so hush-hush about it before. It's never been at such odd hours, and he's *never* refused to tell me whom he's counseling, either."

"What do you want me to do, Cheryl?" *Oh God, not another cheating spouse case.*

"I want you to find out who that hussy is."

"Cheryl, I'm not…"

"If I'm right and I find out first, then they better warm up those prayers they've been practicing because I'll send them to the promised land," Cheryl said.

"Easy, Cuz. I'm sure that even the thought of this must hurt you, but—"

"Oh, Emma, you know I could never hurt a fly. I'm just blowing off steam."

I thought about her reputation for beating up a rival girl in the schoolyard back in the day. She was fifteen years ahead of me in school, so maybe those tales were exaggerated. But fifteen years is a long time for a community to maintain a false memory.

"I can't stand a thief or a cheat, Emma," she said, "That woman might have run off with Frank for all I know. If not, she might know where to find him. You can tell Sam about our conversation, too, if we can trust him not to make it public."

"Cheryl, I'm sorry, but I'm not taking on any new cases. I need a break."

"I know you have your little kayak business, too, but I'll pay you, Emma."

"It's not that, Cheryl—"

42

"Please, Emma. I'm begging you. You're my only hope, and we're family."

****

Most of the time, the hospital parking lot was well-lit, but another dense fog had settled in since I'd entered. The lot appeared deserted, and the Bronco showed up as a dull yellow blur. I walked toward it, and a dark figure ran out from beside it and into the woods.

"Hey, what were you doing?" I yelled, but they didn't slow down.

I ran different possibilities through my mind. Maybe it was their car parked beside mine. So why did they run into the woods? Maybe they'd lost something there earlier and returned to get it. A hubcap might've flown off when they drove by, and they were in the woods looking for it. That was too many maybes for my taste with zero probabilities. My hand slipped back to feel for the comfort of the 9mm, but it wasn't there. It was secured in my lock box under the Bronco's seat—hospital rules.

I grabbed my keys and made a fist with a key wedged between each of my fingers. As I approached the car, I saw the driver's side front tire was halfway deflated. A screwdriver was on the ground beside it. I unlocked my Bronco, jumped in, and took a deep breath—after relocking the door.

I've become such a nervous Nellie. If there was ever a night with the perfect setting for a thriller, this was it. Before I started the car, the pistol was in my lap.

I switched on the headlights and noticed a piece of paper stuck under my wiper blade. After checking in all directions, I wound down the window to retrieve the note. It read:

"Stay away from this case for your own good, but note the striking family resemblance. Miss you, neighbor, Abigail,"

The note made no sense. Abigail? The only Abigail I knew (who also used to be my neighbor) remained locked up in Sykesville Asylum, where she'd been since late last fall. Then there was the part about a family resemblance, but what family resemblance? Unless there were two…

I dialed Sam's cell phone and got his voicemail.

"On my way home," I said, then sent him a text:

—*Sam, I think there may be another murder in Newtowne. Perhaps even a serial killer on the loose. See you soon.*—

I put the Bronco in Drive and pulled out of the parking spot. I circled around the row I was in and aimed my headlights at the woods. A set of eyes shone back at me. I crossed the road to the gas station and refilled my tire. The last thing I needed was a flat tire to top off my day.

Chapter Five

Sam was waiting at the front door when I pulled into my driveway. He started in with the questions before the car was in Park.

"That was a rather cryptic text you sent, Emma. Why do you think there's been another murder? What did Jackie tell you? Are you okay?"

I pulled the note from my denim purse, holding it by the edges with a napkin.

"My prints will be on there from when I pulled it off my windshield, but you might find more."

Sam read the note, a frown creasing his face.

"This is nonsense, Emma. Don't you think? A practical joke. I have no idea what the family resemblance is, and I can't imagine it could be from Abby."

"Unless it's really from the killer, and he's struck again. It's scary, but I must assume it's someone who knows me and about my involvement with Abby's case last year."

"Someone stuck the note on your windshield?"

I described my encounter with the shadowy figure in the parking lot.

"No matter how little sense this note makes, we must take it seriously. Some strange guy hanging around your car runs away into the woods when he sees you. He messed with your tire and left this note, anticipating you being there. Then waits around watching until you leave. This creep has problems. I'm worried, Emma. Always keep protection with you. And why didn't you call me, anyway?"

"I'm not sure it was a man. If so, he was skinny as a rail. And I didn't call because I just wanted to get out of there, Sam. Besides, I'm not defenseless, you know."

"I do know, and if I didn't, you'd remind me. I'm just glad you don't want anything to do with this case. It looks like it might get ugly."

"Oh, umm, I've had a change of heart on that. I'm in now, Sam."

"Oh, Emma. No. Why?"

"They warned me off with that note, and I won't be intimidated. They made a mistake there."

"Not if they know you, Emma. But then again, that might've been their plan all along."

"Either way, it was a mistake on their part. They might not know it yet, but it was."

Sam shook his head and frowned.

"Dinner is almost ready," he said. "I made one of your favorites—hot dog casserole."

"One of my favorites?" I asked.

He smiled. "I warned you I wasn't much of a cook."

"That you did. But you are a virtuoso on barbecue grills and open campfires, as I recall."

He had his back to me and appeared to be scraping burnt beans from the bottom of the pot. I reached up and rubbed his shoulders.

"It's going to be all right, Sam. I'm going to be all right. Besides, you wanted me involved in your cases."

"Not when you've been threatened by the possible

killer in a murder case, Emma."

"Cheryl is family, Sam, so I must help with the missing person's case. I only planned to get Jackie's statement tonight, but now—well, I can't let that thinly veiled threat stand. I won't be intimidated. Do you understand?"

"I understand because it's you, but don't expect me to be happy about it. I'll be worried about you every time you leave the house."

"I don't want you to worry, Sam, but after I eat a bowl of your cowboy special, I'm taking a quick float. I'll only go out as far as McIlhenny Creek."

"By River's End? You want to go back where the body was found?"

"Well, we don't have a cause of death yet on the young woman, and she had no identification with her. Even my teenage girls carried waterproof bags with them kayaking. I'll bet she did, too, until whatever happened to her. Do you think there's a chance that she just drowned? The tide was going out, which might've pushed her into the reeds. I doubt she walked there, so someone must have dropped the body there after the fact. There are many houses adjacent to the creek, too, and it's floatable..."

"It might be worth looking into, although I believe drowning is out of the question. Someone might have helped her drown, though."

I shook my head and bit into Sam's so-called casserole.

"When do we leave?" Sam asked.

"We? You hate kayaking."

"No, I don't. It's just that a skiff is much faster. Slipping in slowly and quietly might be better tonight, though."

"I'll be ready as soon as we finish our fancy gourmet dinner."

"Before I forget," Sam said, "I received two odd phone calls on the landline. It was a local number, but they hung up as soon as I answered. I don't have anything to worry about, do I?"

I recited Cheryl's number from memory and asked if that was who called. He nodded, and I assured him he had nothing to worry about.

"But for me to tell you about that conversation, you have to pinky swear not to tell."

****

"Would you rather two kayaks or one two-seater, Sam?"

"The concept of the two-seater sounds nice, especially for a couple. You know, more romantic and all, working together to reach your destination…"

"But?"

"Yeah, but it's harder to paddle, steer, and awkward. With two kayaks, we can float beside each other and talk without yelling or craning our necks."

"Two kayaks it is then."

Armed with life vests, paddles, headlamps, and high-output flashlights, we slipped the kayaks into the water. I pointed out an occasional crab near the surface and commented on how early jellyfish were in the bay. Sam shrugged his shoulders and paddled on.

"Are you in a hurry, Deputy?"

"Sorry, Emma. I forget that it's the journey and not the destination for you when you're paddling."

He lifted his paddle from the water and stowed it at his side, then hooked our kayaks together and leaned back in his seat.

"I'm fine kicking back with my lady fair on such a beautiful moonlit night. For a bit, let's forget the rest of the world. As far as I'm concerned, it's just you and me, Emma."

"I'm going to make a kayaker out of you yet, Sam."

A whippoorwill called in the distance, and we waited for its mate's answering call. None came.

"Lonely sound, isn't it?" I asked.

"It is. I heard whippoorwills as a kid but haven't heard one in years. I'm seeing why you like this so much, Em."

After some stargazing, we spotted the big and little dippers, and Sam identified the North Star from hiking with the Boy Scouts. That was about the total extent of our knowledge of astronomy. In this case, scientific awareness might diminish the ambiance and romance.

"It's getting late, Emma. Should we paddle for a while?"

"Yeah. It's been nice, but we are on a mission."

Pulling the kayaks through the water with just the strength in our arms, we sent them gliding forward. The bay was still. No boats roared across the water. A lone sailboat slipped along close to shore near the houses in our neighborhood. It felt like we were the first people here. The Song of Hiawatha echoed in my mind. It wasn't the shores of Gitchee Gumee, but it was an experience that the hot rod powerboaters would never know.

"There's McIlhenny Creek, Emma." Sam pointed and turned his kayak toward the opening. We flicked on our headlamps and went in.

The mouth of the creek was broad, and we could paddle side by side. It maintained its width until the second bend when it began to narrow.

"Ladies first," I said, and pulled ahead.

At the next turn, my light reflected off something metallic.

"Sam? There's a canoe."

We pulled our kayaks onto the bank and waded in.

A woman's clutch was on the floor of the canoe. Sam snapped a branch from a hanging maple tree, hooked the bag's strap, and called in our find to the sheriff's office.

"Deputy Douglas, this is Major Mattingley. We have a situation out here on the bay. We found an abandoned canoe...yes, we think it may be related. There's a woman's purse, hoping for ID on the woman...We're on McIlhenny Creek. Yes, that's right. It's out by River's End. Yes, it's the same place...No, on second thought, you wouldn't be able to get the skiff back to where we are. The creek is too shallow. We'll tow the canoe in. Meet us in the van at Emma's. We'll bring it in, but I don't want to use the kayak trailer for transport to the station...Right, don't want to take a chance on any evidence flying out...yes, a full forensics workup."

Sam ended his call and turned to me. "Do you have any rope to tie on the canoe?"

I heard Sam's voice, but my mind was on the woman we'd found. Where did a stranger to our town get a canoe? It seemed likely she was the woman Jackie saw arriving by bus, and the craft had no rental markings.

"Emma? Hello! Are you with me? Is there any

rope?"

"Yeah, I have some in the deck hatch. This is where that young woman met her fate, Sam. Sorry, I've been on the site of too much death lately."

"Yes, we both have, but let's get this canoe out of here. Douglas will be waiting for us at the house. Then we can settle in at home and try to forget this—for tonight, anyway."

****

We paddled slowly and carefully on our way home. The stars had disappeared, and the water was choppy in anticipation of a coming storm. We didn't want to risk the boat capsizing and ruining any potential evidence.

Douglas was already at the house, with the Sheriff's van backed up to the dock. He'd come prepared and had his gloves on. He opened the purse before we pulled the canoe out of the water. He lifted a black leather wallet with a stylized angel etched on the outside.

"It looks like our unidentified woman was named Marsha Johnson, and she was from Charlotte, North Carolina," Douglas said.

"Thanks. Leave the rest until you get everything back to the station and can write up a full inventory. You know the drill."

"No problem, Major. I'll leave a full report on your desk for the morning unless you want an update tonight?"

"Tomorrow will be fine," Sam said.

"By the way, a lot happened after you signed off for the evening, Major."

"Oh? What did I miss?"

"The autopsy results came in. The cause of death

was poisoning. There were remnants of Belladonna berries in the stomach, barely digested."

"That's deadly nightshade, right?" I asked. "How did that happen, do you think? There won't be any nightshade berries out for months yet."

"So, someone must have dried or frozen some from last fall. That makes it murder, not accidental, and premeditated as well," Sam said.

"The coroner thinks that based on the other contents of the stomach, it was administered in a donut or some other pastry," Douglas added. "She said it's bad stuff and only takes about fifteen berries to kill someone."

"Well, that gives us a little more to go on," Sam said. "Did anything else important happen after I left?"

"Not quite as dramatic, but we got the fingerprints back on the breaking and entering at the bakery. There were so many, so I doubt they'll help much, but only three good sets of prints and a partial from the safe area. One matched the shop owner, Katrina Baker, and the other two weren't in the system."

"Interesting," I said. "Kat had that DUI a few years ago, so I guess that's why her prints were on file. If one of the other two did the break-in, they'd be first-time offenders."

Sam helped Deputy Douglas load the canoe and made small talk about office politics. I asked Douglas if he'd like something to drink, but he declined.

"I better get back to the grind, Emma, especially with my boss standing right here."

Sam slapped him on the back.

"I'll see you in the morning before your shift ends," Sam said. "Can you manage the canoe by yourself?"

"No problem. Someone will be around. Nice seeing you, Emma."

The van rolled down our driveway.

"The plot thickens," I said.

"How do you mean?"

"Maybe it's just a coincidence, and I hope so, but Frank Pratt was from Charlotte, also. That's where he met Cheryl. She attended the University of North Carolina for her teacher's certification. He was attending college there as well, until he found religion. Then he changed his major and was accepted into one of the theological seminaries down there."

"Didn't Cheryl say she thought Frank was involved with another woman? Maybe it was someone he knew from down there," Sam suggested.

"I think I need to chat with Valerie and see what she knows and didn't bother to mention."

"The picture of the deceased, Marsha Johnson, will be in today's edition of the County Examiner. At this point, she might not be aware that the deceased was the woman she shared a bus ride with."

"And a ride somewhere in Sofia's car," I added.

"Even still."

"I know. I'm trying not to think the worst of people, but I think it merits a chat with her."

"Don't forget that Cheryl wants to chat with you also," Sam said.

"That will have to wait until tomorrow. It's too late to call now. I'll stop by and speak with her after I talk with Valerie."

"Keep me posted. I'm going to call Sykesville to check on Abby. I want to know who's been in to see her and what special privileges she's been granted, if any."

"You don't think…"

"I'm just crossing the t's and dotting the i's, Em. I'm going to stop in to see Judge Allen, too. I want a search warrant for the bakery. Best place I can think of for Marsha to have picked up donuts."

Chapter Six

Sam left early the following morning. I remember a brief kiss on the cheek and a "Have a nice day" before I fell back into a deep sleep. It was almost nine before I rubbed the sleep from my eyes and greeted the new day. Sam had made coffee, but the pot was cold. I compromised with him on our coffee maker. A standard twelve-cup coffee maker replaced my old faithful percolator. The K-cup style ones were too fancy for my taste, and with the coffee maker, I could still measure the exact dose of caffeine required to get me through the day ahead.

I heated a cup of coffee in the microwave and called the bakery. Kat told me that Sofia and Valerie had taken the day off and gone to the mall. She didn't expect them back until late afternoon at the earliest.

"Do you know the girl Sofia picked up at the bus stop with Valerie?" I asked.

"What girl? Only Sofia and Valerie were there when they came home. Maybe the friend of Val's who was a no-show kayaking? I'll ask Sofia about her if you like?"

"Yes, please. Could you ask one of them to call me when they get home?"

"Of course, Emma. Look, I must run. I'm here by myself today, and the morning rush crowd is starting to pour in."

"Thanks, Kat."

My next call was to Cheryl.

"I was hoping I'd hear from you today," she said.

"I'm sorry, Cheryl. I meant to get back to you last night, but life got in the way. I wanted to make sure you'd be home in, say, an hour or so?"

"I'll be here, cousin."

I sat at the kitchen table and sipped my coffee while doing a few quick searches on the NeighborsSnoop site. Sam advised me not to think the worst of people. Whenever I used this site, though, it was clear how little we knew of the people who lived next door or just down the street. I didn't find much about Marsha Johnson other than her mother's name, Catherine Johnson, and her father's name unknown. I saw nothing incriminating about Valerie Simmons or Cheryl and Frank Pratt.

Pastor Frank and Cheryl lived on the opposite side of town. It was a high-dollar neighborhood with primarily local doctors, lawyers, and old-money residents. The houses were as opulent as my brother's Love's Manor without the history or the leaky plumbing problems. One wouldn't expect such extravagance from a small-town preacher, but their home was on the lot across from Frank's church. I suspected their home was the parsonage and paid for by their parishioners.

Cheryl's door flew open before my finger slipped off the doorbell.

"Good morning, Emma. Come on in. I have coffee."

"Thank you. I had to have a cup before I left the house, but I can always use another one."

Cheryl led me through the house to the dining room, where she had a pot of coffee sitting on a trivet, two cups, and two decanters of cream and sugar.

"Please, have a seat and help yourself, Emma."

"I was surprised to find you at home when I called. I was already looking up the phone number for your florist shop when you answered."

"I have a young girl who comes in several times a week. She's a sweet girl, a little on the privileged side, if you get my meaning. She has work-release at the high school. Some of her classes are in the mornings, and some in the afternoon. I have her come in when she has her mornings free; I'm not a morning person, but she does what I ask and can handle the mornings. I don't go in until the afternoons when she's there."

"School is a lot different than when we went," I said.

"That's for sure," Cheryl answered. "It gives the kids a chance to experience the real world, though."

I nodded. "So, what can you tell me about Frank?" I asked.

"What do you want to know?"

"Everything or anything new. Has he been acting differently lately? Why do you think he's having an affair? Is it only because of that woman he is counseling? When did he last disappear like this? You mentioned he used to be a drinker. Has he disappeared before? Did the two of you have words before he left?"

"Whoa, slow down. One question at a time, Cuz. No, we didn't fight. As for acting differently, he's been distant, and he acts like something is on his mind, something he won't share with me. That's not normal for him. Frank is a talker and loves chatting about his day and parishioners. Now that he's been counseling that woman, though, he won't say a word."

"And has he done this before?"

"It's not something we like to talk about, Emma, but between us, yes. It was a long time ago when he used to drink. It was during our college days that most of that was going on. He'd disappear without a word for several days. I'm not the jealous type, Em, but I thought then he must be seeing someone else. It was just before we graduated, and I told him I was breaking up with him. Frank promised to change if I'd give him another chance. He stopped drinking and never did his disappearing act again—until now, that is."

"Do you know of anyone who has a grudge against Frank? Anyone who'd wish him harm?"

"No, all his parishioners love him. Maybe that woman who he was supposed to be counseling. I'll bet she knows what happened to him."

"And you have no idea who that woman might be, Cheryl?"

"No, I told you, Emma. He was very close-mouthed about her, protective, you might say."

My cell phone buzzed in my pocket. Sam was calling. "Excuse me a second. I need to take this," I said and pressed accept.

"Sam, what's up?"

"Good morning, Em. Have you been to see Cheryl Pratt yet?"

"I'm here with Cheryl now, Sam."

"A couple of things then. First off, we located Frank's car. It's parked at the bottom of the hill by Newtowne Wharf. Straps are lying across the roof like he was carrying something up there."

"Did it look like there was any force used?"

"No, there were no signs of a struggle or blood, nothing like that. It looks like he parked the car and left."

"Okay. What's the other thing?"

"Could you ask Cheryl to come in? We're dusting the car for fingerprints now. We want to get her prints to eliminate them from the equation."

"I'll tell her. I think we're about done here anyway, and I want to stop by the bakery and see if Val and Sofia are back."

"Don't forget we invited Irene and Don for dinner tonight."

"Oh, thanks for the reminder. I forgot all about dinner with them. Any ideas for a menu?"

"We still have some hotdog casserole left over."

"Sam, are you trying to make this the last dinner invitation your sister ever accepts?"

"I think it might be a good night to pick up a party platter from the "Joy of Seafood" restaurant."

"That's a wonderful idea. They both like seafood, right?"

"They live in St. Merriam's County, don't they? Of course, they do." Sam laughed.

"See you tonight, Sam," I said, disconnecting.

I turned my attention back to Cheryl.

"Well, some good news, I hope. They've found Frank's car down by the wharf. That might bring us another step closer to finding him. They are taking prints from inside and outside the car, and Sam asked if you could stop by and let them get a copy of yours."

"Why would they want mine? He didn't run off with me."

"They need yours to eliminate them from the investigation, Cheryl."

"Oh, okay, that makes sense. I'll stop by the sheriff's office before I relieve Savannah at the flower shop."

"Savannah Olsen? Pretty young girl with blonde curly hair?"

"Right. She's the mayor's daughter. Do you know her?"

"Not really. She went on my float trip the other afternoon."

****

The morning rush had thinned out when I got to Baker's Bakery. There was an older, blue-haired lady at the counter paying for her pastries. When she left, the shop was empty except for Kat and me.

"Hey, Emma. I guess you're here for Sofia and Valerie, but they haven't returned home yet. There must've been some great sales up in Chapman County."

"That's okay. There was no rush. I'm sure they'll touch base with me later. You had a good run on the donuts this morning?"

"Every morning, Emma. I've always loved baking, but doing it for a living sure puts a different spin on it. I'm not complaining, though. I'd rather do this than anything else I've tried my hand at to pay the rent."

"I'm glad to hear that. I know how much it means to be doing something you love. It took me long enough. While I'm here, do you mind if I ask you some questions, Kat?"

"Well, sure, I guess it's okay," she said.

"The other day, Sofia mentioned that Pastor Frank came in every morning with the same order. I thought maybe you knew more about that, but you didn't want to be a gossip. But now that he's missing, I hoped…"

"That I'd spill the beans?"

"Well, yes."

"Yes, Sofia was right. For the past week, Pastor Frank has come in for the same order, two jelly-filled donuts, though he claimed he'd only eat one. The other, he said, was for any visitor or secret admirer that might stop by the church. I didn't think much of it until I saw a young woman meet him on the street right after he left here. He held up the bag, and it seemed like it was a routine for them, you know?"

"Did they seem to be close?"

"He hugged her, and she got in the car with him."

"So, you thought…"

"Something was going on? Yes, I did. I thought about it and decided to keep my mouth shut, especially as Cheryl Pratt and I weren't on the best terms. Still, I ratted the preacher out the next time she came in."

"What was Cheryl's reaction?"

"I probably shouldn't tell you this…she's your cousin or something, right?"

I nodded.

"She was livid, Emma. I swear sparks shot out of that woman's eyes so far that I was dialing the volunteer fire department. She said if he were cheating on her after all the years she'd given him, neither he nor his hussy would have many more years left to worry about."

"Oh my, I didn't realize Cheryl could be so aggressive," I said.

"It was probably the heat of the moment, Emma. I'm sure she calmed down."

"I hope so. Can I ask you about something else, Kat?"

She shrugged her shoulders.

"How well do you know Valerie?"

"About as well as we can know anyone, I guess. She and Sofia have been best friends since elementary school, so she's been around the house a lot over the years. Why do you ask, Emma?"

"I'm wondering—does she have a secretive side? Is she one to hide things?"

"Really? This is about her liking girls, Emma? I don't think that's any of my business, and it sure as hell isn't yours either. She and Sofia had a spat around their junior year of high school. I gathered that Val put a move on her. That's the only reason I know. Sofia wouldn't talk about it, but I figured it out. Anyway, two weeks later, they were the best of friends again. If Sofia has no problem with that, I don't either, and neither should you."

"You know me better than that, Kat. I promise it's nothing like that. I was hoping to get a better feel for her before we talked. It's about the woman on the bus she came into town with, and I hope she can help with that. I'm afraid the woman might be the one we found on the bay."

Katrina's face went from an indignant flushed red to a shocked ghostly white.

"Oh, my God." She sat at the counter.

"Are you okay, Kat?"

"You don't think Val…"

"No, I don't think that, Kat. I don't know Valerie at all, but I'm confident she's no killer."

Kat nodded but didn't respond.

"I'm sorry I've upset you, Kat. Are you sure you're okay?"

"I'm fine, Emma. Murders aren't supposed to happen in Newtowne."

I sat with her for a while. We spoke of our old school days, favorite teachers, past boyfriends, and what we'd heard from and about others from our graduating class. When the bell above her door signaled the arrival of a customer, I pointed at the jelly donuts in the display case.

"Do you think I could get a couple of those, Kat? Aren't they the same ones we feasted on yesterday morning?"

"No, you don't want those, Emma. I messed up and used the old batch of filling from my other supplier. I sold one to a teenage girl this morning, and I bet I'll never get her business again. I'm going to throw those out. I'll have some fresh ones with the good stuff out of the oven shortly if you want to wait?"

I opted for two glazed instead and headed to the hospital to share one with Nurse Jackie.

****

As I crossed the parking lot toward the hospital entrance, my phone vibrated, and I saw a text from Sam.

—*Cheryl came in and provided fingerprints. They are a match for one of many sets from the break-in at the bakery. Probably no help.*—

I found Jackie stepping out of a patient's room.

"Hey, Emma, what brings you here?"

"I was in the area and wanted to stop and say hello."

"And what do you have there? Been shopping?"

"It's a thank-you donut. I appreciate the information the other night."

Jackie glanced at the bag. "Baker's Bakery donuts? I appreciate the thought, Emma, but I'll have to decline."

"Why? I know you don't have to worry about your figure."

"It's not that, even though I appreciate your not-so-little white lie...come with me a minute." And down the hall, she went as if in a race. I guess it's an acquired talent that all nurses have. Even the shortest ones can cover a lot of ground in a hurry. She stopped and knocked at one of the patient's doors.

"Come in."

"Miss Olsen, how are you feeling?" Jackie asked.

"Better, Jackie, thank you. Oh, hi, Emma, what are you doing here?"

"I'm fine, thanks, Savannah, but what you're doing here is the better question."

"If you don't mind, tell Emma what you had for breakfast, Miss Olsen."

"I'm embarrassed. I guess you can tell I like my sweets. Well, I stopped by the bakery this morning and got a jelly donut—a blackberry-filled one. Martin and I had one last week, and they were so delish, too good to be honest. I ate it this morning before I opened the florist shop. About the time it touched down, it started coming back up. I was so nauseated. I started shaking and felt dizzy; then my vision became blurry."

"Did you eat anything else or take any medications?" I asked.

"Nope, that was it. I locked up the flower shop, and some nice cop saw me staggering down the sidewalk and brought me here."

"We think it was food poisoning, Emma. Her stomach was pumped out, and the contents will be tested," Jackie said.

"I better go, ladies. Savannah, I'm so glad you're feeling better, and I hope to see you and Martin on the water again soon. Jackie, I'll come up with a better thank-you gift real soon."

"I appreciate the thought, Emma, but unnecessary," Jackie assured me.

I dialed Sam's number on the way to the Bronco, and he answered on the first ring.

"Sam, did you get the search warrant for the bakery? I think it may be the source of the poison."

"We're already here, Emma. On the way to the hospital, I ran into a young lady who convinced me it was a priority."

"Savannah Olsen?"

"Maybe. She was in no condition to chat."

"Okay, I'm headed home. You told Irene six o'clock for dinner, right? Don't be late."

"I'll be there."

Chapter Seven

A quick shower and a change of clothes made me presentable enough for our company—at least family company. I set the table, chilled a bottle of wine, and waited for everyone's arrival.

Don and Irene were the first to grace our doorway. I apologized for Sam's being late, then texted him—a just-in-case reminder. He replied he was en route with the grub from the seafood restaurant.

"You know Sam has never been on time for anything, and men talk about women's punctuality. Hmph! That brother of mine will be late for his own funeral, but I'm sure I don't have to tell you that," Irene said.

Irene's hair was as perfect as ever with its fresh-from-the-salon look, and her quick smile never failed to win me over. She'd let her hair return to its original brunette since I'd been back in Newtowne. A few greys were starting to sneak in, but it added a look of distinction to Irene.

I didn't know her husband, Don, as well. Irene and I grew up together, although several years apart. Don grew up on the other side of the Potomac River in Virginia. We teased him that we might consider him a local if he lived here another fifty years or so.

Don was a banker, and Irene worked for my brother Daniel's lawyer. I can't recall ever seeing either of them in casual clothes. If I ever convinced Irene to come on a float trip with me, I figured she'd show up in business attire.

"What struck you so funny?" Irene asked.

"Oh, nothing. I was thinking about a joke I heard today."

"Well, don't keep us in suspense. Share. We could use a laugh," Don said.

"No, I better not. It's a bit risqué."

"That's okay, we're family," Irene urged.

"Oh, listen," I said. Sam's Mustang rumbled down our driveway.

"You're saved by the bell, Emma," Don said.

Sam burst through the door with four bags of food hanging from his arms.

"Everybody's hungry, I hope?" Sam asked.

"I could eat a horse, and I'm not talking some prissy little colt. I'm talking about one of the Mennonite's draft horses," Don said. "I went easy at lunch so I could come here and eat all your food."

"Let's head to the table then," Sam said. "Can't have my favorite brother-in-law passing out from hunger."

"Yeah, with your favorite brother-in-law also being your only brother-in-law," Irene said.

Irene and I chatted about the books we'd been reading. We both favored mysteries and often exchanged books after we'd read them. The men talked about fishing and this year's Superbowl prospects. Irene filled us in on the latest with their two kids. Missy was in sixth grade this year and was in the school's chorus. Donny Jr. was a third-grader who liked video games too much. Irene said his grades were good, but she had to force him to spend some outdoor time.

Our conversations devolved into work-related themes when the last crab legs were cracked open. I guess that's inevitable once you're indelibly branded as an adult. I tried to recall the exact moment that occurred, but I came up empty. I guess it sneaks up on you.

Don told us about a new housing project that is proposed to be built alongside the Newtowne Wharf. New zoning ordinances were required, and his bank was greasing some palms to make it happen. Irene was animated, describing her new role in Henry Stone's office. Because of her classes at the community college, he'd elevated her to a paralegal position. Irene was still his primary receptionist, but Henry had hired a new girl for her to train.

Sometime after I updated my kayaking business, our dinner went downhill. Sam described some of the events related to the case he was working on while I retrieved one of the blueberry pies I'd picked up at the grocery store. A purchase I didn't mention to Katrina.

"Yes, she was poisoned, and we are exploring all avenues with her. Now that we have an ID, we've contacted the police departments in her hometown. There's a possibility she was known by some of our locals, but I'd rather not speak to that yet." Sam said.

"That poor girl. I feel so bad about it. Her life was cut so short. I feel for her parents, too," Irene said.

"You're right. It was a horrible thing. Everyone keeps saying things like that don't happen here, but they can… anywhere. At least we have an ID on her now, so the investigation is moving forward. It doesn't seem like we've made any progress on Pastor Frank's disappearance, though," Sam said.

"Are you concerned? I mean, do you suspect foul play?" Irene asked.

"With any missing person's case, it's a concern, but Frank Pratt was a long-time resident and didn't appear to be the sort of man to up and run. That's why we're spending almost as much time on his case as Marsha's. Everyone we interviewed today seemed more interested in spreading gossip than in helping to find their neighbor."

"Who did you talk to?" Irene asked.

"There was Mrs. Carole Yates. She claims she heard a big fight from the Pratt's house next door on the evening that he disappeared. She thinks Frank Pratt was seen out with a young woman from the church choir and that he always flirted with the young girls he coaches on the school volleyball team."

"That's sick. Kat's daughter Harper is on that team, and she's fourteen. I hope you didn't believe her. Mrs. Yates is a terrible gossip," I said.

"So, Sylvia Potts informed us. She's another neighbor of the Pratts and claims to be Cheryl's best friend. She said that Cheryl shared her suspicions with her about the possibility of another woman. Sylvia said she'd seen a woman at the Pratt house when Cheryl was out of town. She added that if Frank was cheating, she hated to think what Cheryl would do to the two of them."

"Some best friend she is," Don said.

"Cases like this bring out the worst in people," Sam said.

"When I spoke with Cheryl today, she seemed convinced it had to do with the mysterious woman

Frank had been counseling. She said it was always late at night, and he kept it all hush-hush," I added.

"She thinks he was having an affair with a parishioner he was counseling?" Don asked.

"Yes," I said. "Cheryl said he'd never acted like that on any other occasions or with anyone else, male or female."

"If he'd been cheating before, maybe this time was a first with a married woman," Don said.

"Don't speak ill of the reverend or some woman you don't know anything about," Irene said.

"We're looking into every angle," Sam said. "At least we recovered Frank's car today. We dusted for prints, and we've eliminated his and Cheryl's. There were two other sets of prints. I can't comment on one, and the other set wasn't in the system."

"Oh, my. Look at the time. Don, we really must be on our way. You have an early meeting in the morning," Irene said.

"Irene, you haven't even touched your pie."

"I'm sorry, Emma. I'm sure it's delicious, too, but I'm still stuffed from dinner anyway."

She turned up her glass of wine and polished it off. "Are you ready, my love?"

Don nodded and stood from the table. "It's been a blast, kids. Thank you both for the invite, the excellent food, and most of all, the phenomenal companionship."

Irene kissed me on the cheek. "Always a pleasure, my almost sister-in-law."

"Talk to you soon, brother," she told Sam.

With that, they were out the door.

"What just happened? Did I say something to offend her?" I asked.

"If so, I missed it. I was about to ask you the same thing. Irene has something on her mind and doesn't know what to do about it. I hope everything is okay with their kids."

"I could use a cup of coffee to go with the pie. You want to make a pot of decaf while I load the dishwasher?"

"You're on."

Relaxing at the table, nibbling at our pie, and sipping our hot coffee, we both were lost in our thoughts. I couldn't get Irene's hasty departure out of my mind. They say a Southern person's worst social faux pas is to be rude or inhospitable. People tend to forget that Maryland is well south of the old Mason-Dixon line, and Southern Maryland always felt itself part of the South. Had I been rude or inhospitable?

"Sam, why do you think Irene was upset? I don't think their leaving had anything to do with the lateness of the hour. It's still early."

"What? Oh, I'm sorry, Em. My mind is elsewhere. Irene will be fine. We didn't have anything to do with her leaving so fast. She isn't that thin-skinned."

"So, what's bothering you then, Deputy?"

"That other set of prints I mentioned in Frank's car? The ones I didn't want to comment on? They belonged to the murdered woman, Marsha Johnson."

"That doesn't look good for Frank," I said. "I was afraid the two cases were connected."

"No, it doesn't. If he's out misbehaving somewhere, it would behoove him to show up, and the sooner the better."

"Did any results come back from the bakery samples you took today?"

"No, not yet. We only have the initial mass fingerprints."

"Kat would kill Frank if he hurt her daughter or even if she thought he was acting inappropriately with her. Harper is her world," I said.

"I don't believe that gossip about Frank," Sam said, "but I have to consider it. Even if that were true, though, Katrina would have no reason to hurt Marsha Johnson. If anything, that relationship would draw Frank's attention away from Harper."

"True, and I'm hoping Frank is somewhere sleeping off a bender or whatever, but I can think of only one person who'd have reason to do them both harm."

"Cheryl Pratt, whose friends and neighbors say has threatened violence," Sam said. "I'm asking the judge for a search warrant for her house in the morning."

****

Sam's cell phone rang while we savored our last few bites of pie. His eyebrows lifted.

"It's Irene," he whispered as if she could hear.

"Hey, Sis, is everything okay? Did you forget something here?"

Sam shook his head.

"I can't hear you, Irene. I'm putting you on speaker. Em is here too, so don't talk bad about her."

Sam hit the speaker button as Irene responded. "As if I'd talk bad about Emma. I don't know what she sees in you."

"I can hardly hear you, Irene. Why are you whispering?"

"Okay, I'm going into the bathroom. I don't want Don to hear me."

I looked at Sam, but he looked as puzzled as I was and shrugged his shoulders.

"Drama Queen much, Irene?" Sam asked.

"I apologize for the hour, guys. I know it's late, but I know who Pastor Frank was counseling."

"Do tell…"

"It was me, Sam. I've been seeing him for some months now. Well, not 'seeing him' seeing him, but going to him for counseling, you know?"

"That's nothing to be ashamed of, Irene," I said. "Why wouldn't you want Don to know?"

"It's a long story, Emma, but well, to be blunt, it was about my marriage. I'm thinking of leaving Don." Irene said.

"I don't want to get in your business, Irene, but I'd think you'd be better advised to seek legal counseling in this situation," Sam said.

"If it comes to that, Sam, I will. But I'm hoping we can iron things out and make things work. I thought Frank could help. I wanted someone to bounce my thoughts off who wasn't too close to me socially and wouldn't make my marriage the gossip of the week."

"So, what all the tongue waggers are saying about the pastor and his mystery lady—you, there's no truth to any of it?"

"Are you trying to ask if we were having an affair, Sam?"

"Yes, and the late meetings and the meetings at his house when his wife was away?"

"Boy, you don't pull any punches, do you, brother?"

"I'm sorry, Irene. Maybe you should talk to someone else at the sheriff's office. I don't want to make you feel uncomfortable."

"It's okay. I know it's your job, and I don't have anything to hide except from Don, maybe. Let's see— an affair, no. The late meetings, yes. I didn't want to be seen and gossiped about by going there during daylight hours."

"Did you meet him at his home when Cheryl was out of town?"

"I was getting to that. Yes, I did, but only on one occasion, and I don't know whether his wife was there or not. I can't remember the night, but maybe two weeks back. I don't like to speak ill of him; he was mostly very genuine and kind to me, but not that night. I think he might've been drinking and started telling me how his marriage was rocky, also. He grabbed my arm and shook me, then started spouting off about all the women in his life holding back secrets. When I pulled away, he pretended it was all a misunderstanding. I haven't seen him since."

"Has he tried to contact you since?" I asked.

"Oh yes. A metric ton of text messages. I'd show you, but I deleted them all."

"Was he abrasive, apologetic, or ..."

"Apologetic, Emma. He sent volumes about how much stress he was under and that he'd started drinking again. He said something from his past had come back on him, and he wasn't sure how he felt about it but knew it would destroy his marriage. That's about the gist of the texts."

"Did you ever see him in the company of any young woman, Irene?"

"As opposed to an old woman like me, Sam? No, I never saw anyone like that, and as I said, until that night, Frank was a perfect gentleman."

"Something changed," I said.

"You said several people are referring to a young woman being with him? That's the first time I've ever felt good about being old-er. With all that smoke, there must be fire," Irene said.

"Would you be willing to come downtown and give us an official statement, Irene?" Sam asked.

"I'd rather not, but listen, I hear Don stirring in the other room, so I've got to go. If you really need me to stop by, I'd rather not, but I will, Sam. Bye, guys."

The line went dead.

"What do you make of that?"

"Well, it solves one mystery and shoots down one theory," Sam said.

"Does it?"

"Come on, Emma. It's Irene. You know she didn't do anything to Pastor Frank. But it's looking more and more like he's left town. Besides, even if something was going on between them—which I doubt, what could Irene have against Marsha Johnson?"

"Really, Sam? I bet your contemporaries might conclude that if something was going on between Frank and Irene, then Marsha was the competition. People have killed for less."

Sam didn't respond but stared into his empty coffee cup.

"Look, I don't see Irene harming anyone either. But what would Sheriff Wathen say? If you get Irene to give a statement, he'll be all over her. The least of her problems will be that her secret will be displayed on the front page of the *County Examiner*."

"I guess you're right. What do you suggest?"

"Keep it quiet for now. We will deal with it if it needs to be delved into later. Until then. Let's leave Irene out of it," I said.

"Maybe you're right. I hate the idea of withholding information, but maybe in this case, and we'll have to bring it up if anything else points at Irene."

"Agreed. I haven't run the dishwasher yet either."

"What?"

"You'll need Irene's prints to compare with those in Frank's car. You can pull them from her glass and run them through the database later only if necessary."

Sam nodded his head and stared at the wall.

"Irene had nothing to do with this, Sam. You know this."

He nodded. "You're right. I just hate the thought of her name dragged through the mud."

"Then we need to solve this. I think I'll stop by the school tomorrow. I want to talk to some of the girls on the volleyball team," I said. Sam perked up at the thought of an active investigation.

"Good idea. Before I forget, I called Sykesville today. Abby lost her phone privileges but is still safely ensconced at the asylum. Someone was playing games with that note."

Chapter Eight

Principal Joan Davis was not receptive to my interviewing the students on the volleyball team. I'd hoped to gain insight into the relationship that pastor/coach Frank Pratt had with them. I didn't believe what was being said about him, but Sam thought the kids might open up to me if anything untoward was happening—without it becoming an official inquiry. Speaking with Mrs. Davis, it was apparent I'd need a statement from the sheriff's office, an okay from each parent, and perhaps a notarized document from God before I could speak with the students while on school property.

"I'm sorry, Miss. Please excuse me. I must consider your request, assuming you provide the requisite documentation. But you've caught me at a hectic time. What was your name again?" she asked.

"It's Emma Love, Principal Davis. You might know my brother Daniel?"

"I remember Daniel from school. He thought he was better than those of us who didn't live in a mansion on the hill."

"I believe Daniel has grown older and wiser, especially after the events of last fall."

"Yes, I'd hope so," she said. "Many in our community thought he might be involved with his wife's disappearance. I always liked his wife Gwen. I suppose you're the sister who found her and brought that horrid Abigail Dawson to justice?"

"I'd like to think I helped," I said.

My phone vibrated with an incoming call, but I didn't risk a look.

"Nonetheless, there's nothing I can do..." Mrs. Davis began.

"Major Sam Mattingley asked me to talk with the students, Mrs. Davis. We both hoped to avoid any undue and negative publicity for the school by doing so unofficially. But it's your call, of course. Reporters are printing anything these days."

There was a pause where I heard nothing but a sharp intake of breath.

"Yes, well, there's that. Perhaps I could sit in during these questions? I'd want to ensure our students aren't harassed, and their rights are respected."

"That would be fine if you feel they'll open up to me with their school principal present."

"If that appears to be an issue, Miss Love, we'll address it after I see the direction of your questions."

"Thank you, Mrs. Davis. I want to speak to all the young ladies on the varsity volleyball team individually. When would be the best time?"

"Can you be here in three hours? That will give me enough time to structure your interviews when each student is available or during a subject they excel at. Leave no student behind, you know."

"Thank you, Mrs. Davis. I'll see you then," I said.

****

After disconnecting with the principal, I glanced at my phone to determine why it had vibrated during our conversation. Sam had tried to get a call through to me and then left a text message.

It read, —*We got some interesting results from the fingerprint lab. Give me a call when you can.*—

I called, but it went straight to voicemail.

"Tag, you're it, Sam. I have an appointment at the school in three hours. Taking out the kayak for a little while. Call me back."

I swallowed my last dregs of lukewarm coffee and headed for the kayak rack. If there's a better place to sort through one's thoughts than floating on the water, I'd yet to discover it. The bay was choppy today but deserted. There was one lone skiff working a trotline for blue crabs. I had the rest of the bay to myself. I hoped to paddle out to where the woman's body was found and poke around for a bit. I wouldn't have much time before heading back to shower before my appointment at the high school.

Paddling against the incoming tide was good exercise, though with my tight schedule, I would have preferred calmer seas. I couldn't shake the feeling that Sam and I missed something when we'd found the canoe at McIlhenny Creek. As I approached its outlet to the bay, my phone rang.

"Hey, Sam. What did you find out?" I asked.

"Hi, Emma. I wanted to update you on the fingerprint results we received."

"Well, do tell. Don't leave a girl waiting."

"The canoe we found washed up near where the body was found? Frank Pratt's fingerprints are all over it. Marsha Johnson's prints and someone's not in the system were there, too. Frank's fidelity is looking suspect, Em."

"Frank and Marsha Johnson could both be victims,

Sam."

"I'm keeping an open mind, Emma. This makes the case against Cheryl stronger, though. It gives credence to his affair, and maybe Cheryl's putting a deadly end to it."

"Cheryl was always the jealous type and a well-disguised hothead, but she's no murderer, Sam," I said. "I don't believe all the negativity floating around about Pastor Frank either."

"I know she's your cousin, Emma. If you want to step back—"

"No, I'll see it through, Sam. You know I can be objective."

"Okay. This is the principal direction of our investigation, though. All evidence points in her direction. I'm hoping you'll have a better feel for that after meeting with the volleyball players today," Sam said.

"I understand, Sam. Did you get the search warrant for Cheryl's house?"

"Yes, the house and grounds. The sheriff is out there now, along with two deputies. John said there's a large shed on the back of the property with all manner of dried herbs and berries."

"You know Cheryl minored in botany at college and is a florist, right?"

"One of the dried berry containers was marked 'Atropa belladonna.' It doesn't take much imagination to figure out what that is, but I looked it up to be sure. It's the same poison used to kill Marsha Johnson— deadly nightshade."

"Oh no. I didn't think we even had that here. Dear God. Keep me posted, Sam, and I'll let you know if I find anything out as well."

"Sounds good. Talk to you then. Love you, Emma."

The phone disconnected as I replied, "Love you too…"

It wasn't so long ago that I never wanted to hear those words. Sam was an old flame that sputtered out before I left Newtowne. Not long after I returned, I hoped he'd say them again someday. After months together, I still smiled and felt warm inside whenever the words were spoken.

During our phone call and my daydreaming, the tide pushed my kayak along in its wake. I'd lost half of my progress toward my goal and decided to return home. If I finished my school interviews in time, I'd try again before dark.

****

The first student Principal Davis escorted into the faculty lounge was Katrina's daughter, Harper. Many years had passed since I'd last seen her, and I was amazed at what the passage of time had created. She was a beautiful young woman. Her raven-colored locks flowed over her shoulders. She was tall and shapely, far too much so for a girl her age. For a moment, I pitied her and Kat for the attention she would receive.

"Hi, Harper," I said. "I'm Emma Love, and if it's okay, I'd like to ask you some questions."

"I know. The principal said. I think you're friends with my mom?"

"Yes, Kat and I go back many years. We went to school together here. You look so much like someone I know. I can't place it, and I haven't seen you since you were a toddler."

"My mom. I'm told there's a strong family resemblance. I don't see it myself. What did you want to know, Miss Love?"

"Please, it's just Emma. I hope you'll tell me how you feel about being on the varsity team. You're only a sophomore, right?"

"Yeah, I am, and it's pretty cool. I love volleyball."

"I'm glad to hear that, Harper. I wanted to ask you about the conditions on your team."

"What do you mean?"

"You are a smart young lady, so I'll get to the point with you. Are you ever exposed to unwanted attention from anyone associated with the team or made to feel uncomfortable?"

"Please, no leading questions, Miss Love," Mrs. Davis said.

"It's okay, Mrs. Davis. Do you mean from some of the catty older girls or the boys who are all pervs?"

"I was thinking of anyone older acting inappropriately."

"Oh, so is this about Coach Pratt missing, Emma?" Harper asked.

"Partly, yes."

Harper looked over at Principal Davis. "Would you mind if I speak to Emma alone for a minute, ma'am?"

"Of course not," she said, and stalked out of the room. When the door slammed behind her, I turned back to Harper.

"What did you want to tell me?"

"Well, it's not about coach, but about his wife. Do you know her? She's one batty old witch. I'll bet she did something to coach."

"What makes you say that, Harper? Did Coach

Pratt say something about her?"

"No, the crazy woman accosted me after school a week or so ago. Coach Pratt walked out with us girls. He always does when practice runs a little late and it starts to get dark. Mom wasn't in the parking lot yet; I was the last one there. I could tell coach had somewhere else to go because he kept looking at his watch. Then Mom called me on my cell and said she'd just turned down the street, so I told coach I was good. He said good night and went back inside. As soon as he did, his wife flew up at me in her car and almost climbed the curb. I had to jump back. She yelled at me and called me some nasty names. Then she accused me of doing stuff with coach. I was just like, yuck."

"Were his actions toward you ever inappropriate, Harper?"

"Not at all. I do think I'm one of his favorite players, you know? He gives me extra playing time but never did anything like that. More like a dad, I guess."

"Did you tell anyone about this, Harper? Teachers, your mom, or Coach Pratt?"

Her eyes flitted left and right and finally rested on her high-dollar athletic shoes.

"No. I figured coach had enough on his plate dealing with her."

"Not your mom either?"

"No, and don't tell her, please. My mom worries, and she'd have me living like a hermit. I'm safe. I always have friends with me when I leave school now."

"That's a great idea. Was there anything else, Harper?"

"No, I guess I shouldn't have told you all that. You won't tell her, will you? My mom? She'll think she's to blame."

"Why would she think that?"

She shrugged her shoulders and looked away again. "You know how mothers are, right, Emma?"

I stared at Harper's back as she left the room, and the uncanny resemblance to some unknown person hit me full force. It was Harper's comment about a family resemblance and the same comment in a note from someone masquerading as Abby Dawson. Harper was the spitting image of a younger Marsha Johnson, the murdered woman.

****

Savannah Olsen entered next with Principal Davis, and I stood to shake her hand.

"How have you been, Savannah? It looks like you've recovered nicely from your hospital stay. Are you in playing shape yet?"

"I'm feeling much better than the last time I saw you, Emma, but benchwarmers don't have to be in great shape. I'm the token fat girl, you know. I think Coach Pratt feels sorry for me, and I needed some athletics to join the honor society."

"You're certainly not fat, Savannah, though your height puts you at a disadvantage in your chosen sport."

"It's okay, Emma. I'm fine with who I am. People either like me or they don't."

"Martin certainly seems to," I said.

"Ahem," the principal said. Savannah giggled with her hand over her mouth. I realized Savannah wasn't standoffish as I once thought, only shy.

"Savannah, I'm trying to help the sheriff's office with any leads into your coach's disappearance. Did you hear or see anything that might help us to locate him?"

She turned to look at Mrs. Davis.

"It's okay, Savannah. Anything you say here stays here unless it is something that might hurt you."

Savannah nodded her head and whispered, "Um, I'm not sure if this has anything to do with the coach missing or not, but someone told me he was having an affair with one of the parents here."

"Would you tell me who told you?"

Again, she looked toward Joan Davis, who nodded her head.

"Harper Baker told me."

"Did Harper mention whom she thought the coach was involved with, Savannah?"

"Yes—her mother, Mrs. Baker."

After that revelation, we made some small talk, discussing kayaking, college plans, and even boys. Principal Davis stood up and stepped toward us.

"Will that be all for this student, Miss Love? Savannah has a class she should attend."

"Ugh, Algebra II," Savannah moaned.

She stood, and when the principal turned toward the door, she leaned over and whispered, "Martin needs to speak with you. Will you be around after school? In the parking lot?"

I nodded. "I'll be there."

"He has a rusty brown pickup. You can't miss it," she said.

****

Two more young female volleyball players came and went. Joan Davis soon ushered them both out the door. I then met with Martin's sister, Roxy. We discussed our kayaking trip, but she had no new information to bolster our case. The final young woman was tall and thin, befitting a varsity volleyball player. She was introduced as Laura Bowman, a senior.

"I'm pleased to meet you, Laura. I'm Emma—"

"Love, yes, I know who you are," she replied. Her look seemed to indicate an unpleasant familiarity that I was unaware of.

"I'm sorry. Do we know each other from somewhere?"

"No, but I know who you are. You're the private detective who sent my boyfriend's mother to jail. Now he's in foster care."

"You mean Jack Dawson, Abby's son?"

"Have there been that many families' lives you've ruined that you have to ask, Emma?"

"I'm sorry you feel that way, Laura. I'm sorry about Jack, too, but he'll be eighteen soon and out of the system. I did some checking, and the Dawson house is paid for. Jack will have a place to stay. My brother Daniel hired a cleaning crew to clean it for him, and his maintenance guy is keeping the place up so it will be ready for Jack on his birthday. I've put out some feelers, and the day he turns eighteen, he will have at least two job opportunities. There's a lot of goodwill toward Jack in the community, Laura. As for Abby, she is where she needs to be for now. She's getting help there."

"Oh, I didn't know. When Jack asked me to…," she started.

"What did Jack ask? Is it something I can help with?" I asked.

"Oh, it's nothing, never mind me. It's a personal thing."

Again, I had a teenager in front of me who wouldn't make eye contact. These kids hid so many secrets, but I left it alone.

"I'm here to investigate the coach's disappearance, Laura. I suppose you ladies spent as much time with him as anyone. I hope you know something that will lead us to him."

"There's at least one somebody who knows him much better than any of us do." Laura smirked.

"Who might that be?"

"I don't know who she is and shouldn't say anything. Jack said to stay out of it, or his family would somehow be blamed."

"Blamed for what, Laura?"

"Look, the other evening, I saw coach in town. He had a woman with him, a not-his-wife woman, if you catch my meaning? At first, I thought nothing of it though. It looked like Harper Baker when he got out to open the car door for her. I figured Mrs. Baker ran late and hadn't picked her up from school. When the woman stepped around the car, though, I saw it wasn't Harper. This woman was older but still way too young for coach."

"What were they doing? Did you see where they went?"

"I couldn't say for sure, but they were being plenty sneaky about it. Her dark grey hoodie was pulled down over her eyes. He had on a baggy sweatshirt and an old Ravens ballcap pulled down low. I'd say they weren't up to anything that a pastor ought to be caught doing."

"That's very interesting, Laura. I appreciate you sharing what you saw. It might help us find the coach."

"Are you sure he wants to be found?" she asked.

"We are assuming so, Laura. There's nothing to indicate otherwise. Was there anything else you noticed? Anything that seemed odd, maybe?"

"Well, it was already getting dark, and kind of late to be having a picnic or to go canoeing."

"A canoeing picnic?"

"Yeah. I'd never seen Coach Pratt strap a canoe on top of his car before, and he was carrying one of those big picnic baskets you see in the old movies. I've only seen them in the romance stories that my mom watches when my dad is out of town. And, oh yeah, he had a waterproof yellow tote with him, too. He put it and the basket in the back seat."

"Did you see which way they went?" I asked.

"I was being nosy, so yeah, I watched until they were out of sight. I think the coach saw me and skidded tires when he pulled out. They drove toward Newtowne Wharf."

"Is there anything else, Laura?"

"No, I think that's all I can remember."

"Would you call me if you think of anything?" I handed her my card. She glanced at it and jotted my number on her notebook.

"I'll call you, Emma, but I won't take your card. Jack might see it, and I don't think he's ready to see you as one of the good guys yet. You won't tell him about our conversation, will you?"

Laura left soon after, and Mrs. Davis closed the door behind her.

"I think Laura must be the last one for today, Miss Love. The bell for the last period is about to ring. I must say you have a way with the students. You got more out of Laura than her teachers have all year. Did you ever consider teaching?"

"No, but I like young people; maybe they can tell," I said.

"Do you think you'll need to come back? There are only two more girls to talk to. I can give you their names if you'd consider speaking to them off campus?"

"That would be fine. Thank you, Principal Davis."

The bell rang, and I grabbed my notes and headed for the parking lot to meet with Martin Jackson.

The hallway was filled with departing students. Like the volleyball players, many of them wore white Varsity jackets. I thought they looked just like the one the river shooter had worn.

Chapter Nine

The parking lot had all the hallmarks of a drag racing venue. Cars zipped back and forth with little concern for pedestrians or fellow drivers. The air was filled with the scent of exhaust fumes, burning rubber, and the sound of squealing tires. It would not have seemed out of place if a teacher was waving the checkered flag.

A beat-up brown truck whipped by, and the driver waved. I couldn't tell for sure if it was Martin behind the wheel, but I saw crab pot traps stacked high in the back. In a minute, the packed parking lot had emptied. The only motion was from late arrivals toting stacks of books to their cars. Seeing them reminded me of the many occasions in my school years when I should have cracked the books instead of playing in the river. But I didn't regret a thing.

My phone rang as I walked toward my Bronco.

"Hey, Sam. How's everything going?"

"Not the best, Emma. I've been trying to talk John out of getting an arrest warrant for Cheryl Pratt. He's adamant she's our killer."

"Don't you think that's a bit premature?"

"I do, and so far, he's going along with me, but I'm not sure for how long. Another straw will break the proverbial camel's back."

"I wonder if Kat ever mentioned Frank's standard

donut order to her?"

"What?"

"Nothing…sorry, I'm just thinking out loud," I said. "Was anything interesting discovered from the search warrant at the bakery?"

"Nothing yet, or no results yet anyway. We took samples of all the jelly bucket containers, including one hidden in the back of the refrigerator. Katrina didn't seem happy that we took a sample from that one. She claimed she couldn't find it after the break-in, and when she did, it had an expired date. The bucket was almost empty, and a spoon was inside, so we took that too. Katrina said it was jelly filling from a supplier she didn't use anymore; she meant to toss it out."

"Interesting. I'll have a lot to fill you in on tonight. Some of the volleyball players were very forthcoming. I took notes," I said.

"Okay, I'll see you tonight then."

As soon as my call with Sam ended, my phone buzzed immediately. I glanced at it to see a voicemail was received. I slid into the Bronco's driver's seat to listen.

"Hi, Emma, this is Sofia. Katrina said you were trying to reach Valerie. Her phone is dead, so I wanted to let you know we continued north on our shopping trip. We are staying in the big city for the weekend. Was there something important? Hopefully, it can wait until we get back. Val was supposed to meet someone here who hasn't shown, so we're checking out the nightlife tonight. Woo Hoo!"

I considered all the information I'd received from the volleyball players and Sam's update, then tried to return Sofia's call. It also went to voicemail:

"Hey, Sofia. All is good. I think we're close to wrapping it up here. I appreciate you reaching out. I will talk to you when you get home. Tell Valerie I said hello, and you guys have fun!"

****

I drove home, changed clothes, and went to my garden. I was worried about my broccoli plants. Some were already forming heads and were far too small to amount to much. I regretted not having watered them during our early dry spell. The marigolds I'd planted around the border of my tomatoes were flourishing. Marigolds would always take the grand prize if there were an award for a beautiful, no-care-needed flower. I chopped a few sprouting weeds around the lettuce plants and hilled some soil around my tender young tomatoes.

I thought of Nana Love and how much she loved fresh garden tomatoes, almost as much as she hated the "hothouse" ones, as she called them. I'd be sure to take her some from the first picking. With dementia weighing heavily upon her, she might not remember my visit, but she'd remember the tomatoes.

I knelt by the flower bed near the house and began to pull up some stubborn crabgrass. Halfway through, thoughts of the case intruded on my happy place. I put the hoe away in the shed and went inside to my laptop. I couldn't shake the sound of metal thumping as Kat climbed out of the kayak that auspicious night. Then there was the oversized sweatshirt she'd worn on a warm night. It was odd for a woman who had never worn an oversized anything.

I signed in to the website "NeighborsSnoop" and began my queries. I found Katrina Baker's application for a handgun, a 9mm automatic. Could she have slipped away from us only to shoot the warning shots? Was she aware there was a body dumped in the reeds? I tried another search but found nothing registered to Cheryl Pratt. Frank Pratt was a different story. Last year, he purchased a .380-caliber pistol. To assume that Cheryl also had access to it wasn't much of a stretch.

My search did nothing to narrow the suspect pool. I decided a shower would clear my head before I started dinner. It looked like Sam's day would be a lot longer than mine.

As I shut the door to the bathroom, the house landline rang. I decided the probable telemarketer would have to wait. That was the norm on the landline.

The shower was refreshing but did not provide the clarity I had hoped for. I slipped on a robe as I dried my hair and headed to the kitchen, passing by the landline on the way. The message light was blinking.

"Okay, let's hear all about what you're trying to sell me today," I said with my finger poised over the delete button.

"Miss Love, I mean Emma, this is Martin Jackson. I'm sorry I had to run today, but—Miss Love, I think I'm in trouble, and it's something terrible. Can you please call me back? It's really important."

I heard another voice in the background that sounded like Savannah.

"Tell her what you found, Marty...." Then the phone beeped, and the call died.

****

I checked the number and dialed it from my cell phone. Savannah answered on the first ring.

"Is this you, Emma?" she asked.

"I just got Martin's message, Savannah. What is going on? Are you and Martin okay?"

"No, not really. Can you come out to the point? There's something you should—there's a dead body out here, Emma. We think it's Coach Frank, and there's a lot of money…"

"Where are you, Savannah?" I asked.

"Martin says we're past Fisherman's Point by a green buoy. It has the number seven stenciled on it. You had better hurry. The body is about to be swept into the Potomac, and the river is rough this afternoon. I think there's a storm coming."

"Okay, don't let the body float into the river, but try not to touch anything. I'll take the neighbor's johnboat and be there soon," I said.

I ended the call and dressed while I was dialing Sam.

"Hey, Emma," he answered. "How's it going?"

"Look, Sam, I must be quick. Two teenagers found a dead body floating out by Buoy #7. They think it's Frank Pratt. That's not far from Fisherman's Point and close to the river. They said the body was about to be swept out into the Potomac. I'm taking Mr. Jenkin's johnboat. Meet me."

I heard Sam's "No, Emma, it's too rough," but didn't wait for any further response. I slipped on my shoes and headed for the dock. The gas tank was half full—enough to get me there and back. The second pull on the starter rope and the engine roared to life. The 25-horsepower outboard motor moved me across the water much faster than I was used to in my kayak, and I soon regretted not wearing a light jacket in the rough seas.

When I was halfway across the bay, I could already

see their boat anchored and waiting. I twisted the throttle, but I was already maxed out. The closer I got, the darker the sky became. We were in for a bad storm. I momentarily thought of my tender young tomato plants and hoped they'd weather the coming winds. Heat lightning lit up the darkening sky. We'd have to move fast. Where was the sheriff's boat?

I cut back the throttle as I pulled alongside Martin's workboat. The smell of death and decay was unmistakable despite the north wind picking up.

"Thank God, Emma," Savannah yelled over the sound of my motor. "We looped a rope around his boot. He's not going anywhere."

"Great job, both of you. Is this where you found the body?"

"Maybe fifty yards or so that way." Martin pointed. "He was drifting fast before we tied on to him and anchored the boat."

I threw a rope toward Savannah. She pulled the johnboat closer and tied my mooring rope to their gunnel.

Martin held the boats steady, and I climbed over into their boat. A second rope on the opposite side of the boat was pulled taut, and I glanced over at the grisly sight attached to the end of it. The body was floating face down. It looked like Frank Pratt.

Savannah was as white as a sheet in a five-star hotel. Martin looked in the direction of the approaching storm.

"Looks like we're in for a gulley washer, Emma," he said. "Did you call in the police?"

"I did. They should be here soon. I think I should take Savannah home, Martin. Her parents will be worried, and yours will, too."

"I don't know. This is a lot more boat than your little johnboat. I wouldn't want to be out here in that if the water gets much rougher."

I heard a large outboard's roar as it left the Newtowne Wharf. The encroaching darkness made them use their lights, and I suggested Martin turn his on, too.

"I'm betting that's Sam coming now. It looks like the sheriff's boat lights. Once he gets here, I want the two of you to head straight home. No excuses," I said.

Martin moved forward to switch on his lights, and I noticed a yellow waterproof bag beside the boat controls. I remembered Harper's comment about Frank carrying one just like it.

"What's in the bag?" I asked.

Savannah cleared her throat and stared at Martin. "He was supposed to talk to you about that after school today."

"I couldn't help it. Sorry, Emma. My dad called and told me to come straight home. He needed me to check our crab pots before this weather moved in. Mom's been sick…"

Martin walked over to the bag, unzipped it, and pulled it open for me to see. There were at least ten banded packs of hundred-dollar bills, a minimum of ten thousand dollars.

I'm sure my eyes were as big as saucers, and it took a moment to catch my breath.

"Where did you find this, Martin?"

"It was up on the side of the bank on McIlhenny Creek. There's like a small clearing there. We found something else there, too."

Martin stepped into the cabin and brought out an old-fashioned wicker picnic basket.

"This was up there, too. Not much inside, though. Guess somebody had their picnic already."

"You shouldn't have touched any of it, Martin. Fingerprints..."

"Go on, Martin," Savannah said. "Now tell her why you and Jerome were up there to start with."

Martin looked at his feet and scuffed his shoes against the bottom of the boat.

"We didn't know it was you, Emma. Honest. Some thief's been stealing crabs from our pots..."

"Whoa, start at the beginning, Martin," I said.

"We have a string of crab pots where the creek dumps into the bay, you know? Crab traps?"

I nodded.

"Somebody's been sneaking out there at night and stealing all the crabs out of them. They're easy to find because they're marked with our small orange Styrofoam buoys. We have our identifying numbers carved into them. You've seen them, I'm sure."

Again, I nodded. "Go on, Martin."

"My dad asked me to go out that night to scare away any thieves that showed up. I called Jerome, and he wanted to come along, like on an adventure. Before dark, we found that bag full of money. We wanted to go home and tell our folks, but we decided to wait in case the thieves showed up."

"Did they?"

"We didn't know it was you, Emma. We heard the paddling and figured that's just what a thief would do to be quiet, and I shot my dad's pistol to scare them off. Well, you, as it turned out."

"Martin, you shot at us? You nearly hit me!"

"No, ma'am. You must understand that those crabs are our livelihood, but I know better than that. You never shoot at the water; the bullet can ricochet…"

"Then why did you?"

"I shot up in the air, and they were blanks anyway. When I shot, Jerome threw a big rock into the water at the same time to run the thief off. We didn't know it was you, Emma. I'm sorry we scared you. Then we heard about the body being found, and we were afraid to tell anyone about the money. We thought maybe it was a drug deal that had gone bad, or a mafia hit. But that's all we did. We didn't kill anybody."

"Nobody will think you did, Martin," I assured him. "The woman was dead for a while before she was found."

"See, Martin, I told you Emma would help," Savannah said.

Distracted, we only became aware of the sound of the sheriff's boat seconds before its searchlight flashed over us.

"Emma," Sam yelled.

****

Deputy Douglas and Sam used padded oyster tongs and a makeshift gurney to pull the body from the water. It was Pastor Frank Pratt.

I filled them in on everything Martin and Savannah told me, including the money bag.

"How much did you handle it, Martin?" Sam asked.

"Some, sir. Mostly, the handle part. We took some of the money out but didn't break the bands. We'd never seen that much money before."

"Who is the 'we' you are referring to?"

"Me and Jerome. We found it. We didn't know about the dead woman," Martin said.

"Jerome, who?" Sam asked.

"Jerome Somerville, Sam. He's Nurse Jackie's brother," I answered.

"I'll need you and Jerome at the sheriff's office tomorrow morning for fingerprinting. Should I contact your parents, or will this request suffice?" Sam asked.

"No. Sir. I mean, yes, sir, we'll be there."

"Okay, you kids go home before this weather worsens. Be safe, and I'll see you tomorrow, Martin," Sam said, then turned to me.

"Hop in, Emma. We'll tow the johnboat back before you get caught in the storm or old man Jenkins reports it stolen.." Lightning flashed to punctuate his words, and I climbed in.

Chapter Ten

When Sam docked the boat at the house, the rain was torrential. The gale-force winds joined forces with the raging seas, and our boats bounced like two rubber duckies in a sugar-fueled toddler's bathtub. It took all our efforts to secure the boats to the dock pylons, and then Sam, Douglas, and I dashed for the house. It made no difference. Unless able to dodge the raindrops, a good soaking was inevitable.

Sam grabbed the waterproof money bag, and Douglas carried the picnic basket. We had to leave poor Frank lying in the bottom of the boat. It made me sad even knowing that he was past such worries. Halfway up the hill, Deputy Douglas lost his footing in the wet, muddy grass and slid several feet on his backside. Somehow, he managed not to drop the picnic basket Martin and Jerome had found. Sam grabbed him under his arm, and we all moved on.

I dared a glance toward my garden, but the rain blasted me in the face. I could only hope that the embankment above my plantings and the evergreens near the shore would provide enough windbreak that my efforts weren't destroyed.

"Emma, I can't go inside like this," Douglas said as we reached the sanctuary of my covered porch. "I'll track water everywhere, and I'm all muddy too. I can just wait out here under the porch roof. This deluge won't last long."

"Nonsense, you'll do no such thing. Get in here, out of the weather."

Two lightning bolts converged from opposite directions and struck a tree at the water's edge. The maple split in half as if hit by Paul Bunyan's axe. I felt the porch floor tremble from the force. The explosion left us all with ringing ears.

"Now, Douglas," I said.

I ushered the two men inside; Douglas was reluctant but compliant for now.

"Sam, would you grab a couple of flashlights and the kerosene lantern in case the power goes out? They're on the shelf in the laundry room. I'll make us some coffee. One of the benefits of a gas stove is we'll get our coffee regardless."

"Sounds good," Sam said. "Douglas, I'm going to grab us some dry clothes first. I think we're about the same size. We'll be off duty before this rain stops, anyway."

"There's no need to go to all that trouble, Major. I'll dry out in a bit." Douglas squatted by the door, unlacing his shoes.

"No trouble at all, Deputy. I don't think I have any footwear that will fit those boats of yours, though. You'll just have to hang out in your stocking feet until the weather breaks."

"What is that stuck on your shoe, Doulas?" I asked.

"Oh, I don't know. Picked up a scrap of paper, it looks like." He lifted his shoe and peeled off the paper. "Where's your trash can?"

"Let me have it," I said. The paper was folded twice, and I saw blurred ink printing.

"What is it? A coupon from a burger joint or something?" Sam asked.

"No, I think it's a note…let me see if I can make it out."

I read it out loud, "Dear Emma, your buddy has been cooking up more than donuts. Ask her about the kid's daddy. Hugs, Abby."

"Abby who?" Douglas asked. "The only Abby I know from around here is committed to the asylum where she belongs."

We filled him in about the previous note, which was signed by someone claiming to be Abby or perhaps someone acting on her behalf.

"What is this note referring to, Emma? Any clue?" Sam asked.

"I can't say for sure, but I'm guessing Katrina and Harper Baker. I had some interesting conversations at the high school today. Among other revelations, it seems that Harper is the spitting image of the murdered woman, Marsha Johnson. Someone may be trying to make a connection. I'll tell you about it in a bit, but first, I need to call Martin to ensure they got home okay. They were far enough ahead of us to beat the worst of the storm, but I want to check on them."

"Meanwhile, don't you have an old fingerprinting kit around here somewhere, Emma?" Sam asked. "The money bag and picnic basket will give Douglas and me something productive to do."

****

After speaking with Martin on his cell, I returned to the kitchen. My table was covered with spread-out newspapers. The men stood over the picnic basket and money bag. The contents of both were dumped on the kitchen counter. I stared at the men's gloved hands and tiny brushes and stifled a laugh. It looked like a scene stolen from a hospital soap opera.

"Shouldn't you both be wearing scrubs and surgical masks?"

"No, ma'am," Sam said. "This is just the pre-op examination—I mean investigation."

I slipped on my gloves and thought about Laura Bowman's embarrassed comment. Something that she wouldn't have done if she'd known we were trying to help her boyfriend, Jack Dawson. A deed that was done at Jack's request. Then she clammed up and became distant. I wondered whether Laura was the writer of the notes or just the deliverer. I was convinced she was one or the other, if not both.

****

While Sam and Douglas brushed their magic black fingerprint powder over the containers, I moved to the kitchen counters and dug into their contents. The money bag held exactly ten grand in hundred-dollar bills. Like the kids, I didn't break any of the bands. Nothing else was in the pile from the waterproof bag (although ten thousand dollars was interesting enough).

Next were the items from the picnic basket. The first things I retrieved were two plastic sandwich bags. One was marked "M—ham and cheese with mayo," and the crusts from the sandwich were still inside. The other bag was empty and marked "F—ham and cheese with mustard." I was pleased to see they planned to take their trash out when they left their picnic spot, even though they never got the chance.

"You'll want to print these, Sam," I said, holding up the bags.

He gave me the thumbs-up, but his eyes never left his work.

There was an empty bottle of wine from our local vineyard. I suspected any prints rendered from it would include Martin's and Jerome's.

Next was a plastic grocery store bag adapted as a trash receptacle. It held napkins, wet towelettes, an empty potato chips bag, and two candy bar wrappers. Two red plastic cups were included and also marked "F" and "M": Frank and Marsha.

I recognized the last item as a repurposed margarine container when I opened the lid.

"Sam, you guys better look at this," I said.

"What is that stuff?" Sam asked.

"Looks like jam," Douglas said.

I looked closer and saw remnants of dark berries mired in a syrupy concoction.

"If I had to guess, I'd say it's a blackberry compote," I said.

"A what?" The men echoed each other.

"It's like jam but chunkier and cooked down in the syrup. Most folks eat it over pancakes, yogurt, or waffles, but it's good on its own."

"Well, under different circumstances, it would look good."

"You can't eat the evidence, Deputy Mattingley."

"I wasn't, Emma. I *am* getting hungry but not that hungry."

"There isn't much of it left. It must've been good. You'll definitely want prints off this."

"And an analysis of the contents," Sam said. "I hope they can scrape enough off to use. If I recall correctly, the lab requires 25 grams or just under an ounce for definitive food testing."

"That might be pushing it, Sam. One side looks like it was licked clean."

****

The weather cleared before we finished our kitchen science projects, and the sun came out in time to provide a spectacular multi-hued sunset. The three of us walked down to the dock together. Sam and Douglas had bagged all the evidence from the two containers and loaded them on the Sheriff's boat. Thankfully, the tarp we'd tied over Frank Pratt's body remained in place.

"I'll be back, Emma. I think we've all put in a long enough day already," Sam said. "As soon as we dock the boat at the wharf, we'll head to the office with the evidence, grab our vehicles, and then head home."

"No passing 'Go' and no collecting two hundred dollars?" I asked.

The men waved as they throttled forward in the now mirror-smooth bay.

I swung by my garden before I went inside. The tomato plants had a few broken branches, but their young and supple stems bent with the winds instead of snapping. Flexibility trumped rigidity. I could take a lesson from those tomatoes.

Some broccoli plants lay toppled, their roots exposed. Before the roots could dry out, I set them upright and scuffed some wet soil over them with my shoe. My just-sprouted corn was laid flat. I'd have to replant those four rows. Along the garden's border, my ever-faithful soldiers, my marigolds, stood as robust and colorful as ever.

I went inside to wait for Sam. It would take him a

while to arrange transport for Frank's body to the Medical Examiner's Office in Baltimore. He'd said, 'straight home' and probably meant it, but I knew Sam. He'd take it upon himself to deliver the news to Cheryl about Frank's death. Then, he would have a few reports to write up before he could call it a day.

I texted him. —*If you are going to break the news to Cheryl, I can lend moral support. I'll be there if you need me. Just let me know.*—

I carried my laptop into the kitchen and clicked on my favorites—the top one, NeighborsSnoop. It took a moment, but the reliable site soon gave up the name and phone number of Jack Dawson's guardian. She picked up on the second ring.

"Hello, Mrs. Parker. My name is Emma Love. I'm helping the sheriff's office with an inquiry, and I was wondering if I could speak with Jack Dawson."

"The sheriff's office, you say? What has that boy gone and done now? I swear this foster parenting ain't what it's cracked up to be. Little hoodlums are always stealing something from the house or causing mischief in town. Then my neighbors look at me like it's all my fault. Their misbehavior reflects on me, after all."

"Yes, ma'am. I understand. I can see where that could be frustrating. Still, if I could speak with Jack?"

"Yes, hold on, and I'll grab him for you. He didn't hurt anybody, did he? Just wondering after that mother of his…"

"No, ma'am, but I think he can help with our investigation."

I heard Mrs. Parker scream Jack's name, loud enough to alert neighbors several houses away. I suspected they heard her often and wondered how they felt about that.

"Hello," Jack said.

I decided to play my hunch.

"Hi, Jack. I hoped to speak to you one-on-one this way to avoid any police involvement."

"What's that 'sposed to mean, Miss Love? I ain't done nothing."

"You haven't done anything serious, Jack, but I want to ask about the notes you've written to me and signing your mother's name."

"I didn't give you no notes. My mother is in jail, if you recall."

"I know you didn't leave them. I believe you had your girlfriend do that, Jack. Do you think that was wise? Laura seems like a very sweet girl."

"Yes, she is, but leave her out of this."

"Look, Jack, I didn't call to harass you or to get you or Laura in trouble, but…"

"But what? What do you want?" he asked.

"If you give me a chance, I'll lay all my cards on the table now, or I'll ask Sam to pick you up so we can do it in a more formal setting. It's your call, Jack."

"Go on then. What do you have to say?"

"I've received a pair of notes concerning the case I'm currently helping with. The author of those notes appears to have known some things about this case before we did. I'd like to know if they know anything else, and I'd like to know the source of the notes."

"You said my mother signed them. Why don't you ask her?"

"I've known Abby for a long time, Jack, since before you were born. She often talked about her school years at a private school and how strict the religious clergy was. Your mother was a Southpaw, but her teacher thought being left-handed was sinful. She said it was the devil's hand. Whenever Abby picked up a pencil or a crayon with her left hand, they'd crack her on the knuckles with a thick ruler. Eventually, they broke her from using that hand for her schoolwork. Abby writes right-handed now, although it's straight up and down and doesn't slant to the right like most right-handers. On the other hand, pardon the pun; you are left-handed, and your writing has a distinct leftward slant, just like on both notes you left for me."

"So what? Ain't no crime against writing a note, is there? We still got freedom of speech in this country."

"I just want to know the source of the information, Jack. Did Abby tell you what to write and to give it to me?"

"Yeah, okay. I guess. My mom says you're her favorite neighbor, but I don't know why. You put her in that asylum, but she wanted you to know. She said you were honest and did what you thought was right, but you didn't always pick up on her clues."

"What clues are those, Jack?" I asked.

"Mom said it's been brewing a long while with Mrs. Pratt and Mrs. Baker and that things would be coming to blows if something worse didn't happen first."

"Why does she think that, Jack?"

"I reckon from the notes and what's happened that it's about those two women fighting over something— maybe the preacher? I think Mrs. Baker's daughter Harper is involved somehow. Whenever I asked my mother about any of it, she'd say they would pay the wages of sin for the sins of their fathers. You know how

Mom talks when she gets all religious. She said I didn't need to worry over it."

"Thank you, Jack. I appreciate your time and honesty. You take care of yourself and that young lady of yours. Maybe you could come by sometime, and I'll take you both out on the kayaks. That is if you want, and it's okay with Mrs. Parker. Abby always said you loved being on the water."

"I'm not sure how that would look, Miss Love."

"Well, you think about it, Jack. You'd be welcome, and I think Abby would approve."

****

The conversation went better than anticipated. True, I hadn't acquired any earth-shaking information, but at least I knew Abby was the source. As the primary supplier of gossip in our small town for so many years, I was sure there were plenty of secrets she could reveal.

I wondered if it was too late to call Sykesville Asylum to pick her brain, but headlights turned into my driveway. I peeked out the front window as Sam stepped out of his Mustang with his gym bag in hand. I met him at the front door.

"I didn't know if I'd see you tonight, Sam, but the gym bag tells me you plan to stick around. How was Cheryl? You stopped and saw her? Told her…"

"Yes, sorry it took me so long. I hoped it might be easier for her, coming from someone she knows a little. It was about as you'd expect. I felt so sorry for her. It's far from my first time breaking such horrible news to someone about a loved one, but it never gets easier. I remember every one of them. I'll never forget the look on their faces when reality smacks them. Some collapse on the spot. I've caught a few in mid-fall. Others scream hysterically, and their tears flow like an overflowing dam. It's the other ones that are the worst. Ones like Cheryl. They stand there, and you can see the emotion build like a balloon blown up too far and about to pop. But they don't. They pull it all back in, suck it in like a vacuum, and store it in a steel-reinforced concrete box. There's a disconnect in their eyes, but you know the piper will be paid. It's just a matter of time before the horror strikes them down."

"I'm sorry, Sam. It must have been awful for you. Both of you."

"Worse for Cheryl, but I'm fine. Do you mind checking in on her tomorrow?"

"Of course. First thing I'll run by."

"Good. I'm turning in shortly, Emma. It's been a long day. Could we catch each other up and call it a night?"

"Sounds good to me," I said.

Chapter Eleven

I didn't remember falling asleep or anything else after my head hit the pillow. The next thing I recall was Sam kissing me on the cheek and suggesting we meet for lunch. I was confused at first why he'd want to discuss lunch in the middle of the night, but a glance out the bedroom window confirmed a new day's dawn.

"Sure, text me where you want to meet later," I said.

I heard the Mustang roar to life outside, then the crunch of tires on the gravel driveway. Every sound seemed magnified, the cardinal chatting it up on the windowsill and the flicker pecking at the wooden eaves of the house.

As often happens when I've felt despair, my departed sister Maya spoke in my head.

"Don't doubt yourself, Emma. You'll figure it out. You were always the best at puzzles..."

"I've hurt so many, Maya, including you. If I'd been faster—if I'd seen..."

"You were a child, my baby sister. You've given me peace and stopped Abby from hurting anyone else."

"I've ruined lives! Our cousin Cheryl is my latest victim."

"You've always been too hard on yourself. I know how brave you are, Emma, but you tend to forget. Find out the truth, whether it be friend, family, or foe. Make

it right, Sis. Only you can."

"Who should I be looking at? There are so many motives…" But it was too late. The fog in my mind cleared. The crows started cawing outside my window, pulling me back to reality. It was time to think about Cheryl and the shock she'd experienced. I needed to stop in and see if she was okay and if I could do anything to help.

Rise and shine. No more sleep for you today.

Coffee and a busy day ahead were waiting. The coffee came first, and I smiled to see the half-pot that Sam left in the coffee maker. It was still hot enough to burn my tongue when I took a hurried first sip. A shower and casual dress followed the caffeine and the stale donut.

I tried Cheryl's phone before leaving but received no answer, and her voicemail was full. Her house was a few minutes out of the way from just about everything, but I decided to try a drive-by to see if she was home.

I turned the Bronco around in the driveway, and as I slipped it into Drive, I saw a familiar figure. Our once-local reporter, Johnny Walker, stood alongside his small black station wagon. The rattle-can spray paint job had seen a do-over. The bald tires were replaced with new treads, but it was Johnny's car all right. The blacked-out rear and side windows gave the vehicle a mini-hearse look. I'd mentioned to Johnny before that his ride looked like a prop for a pet cemetery.

"What brings you here, Johnny? I thought you were writing for the competition on the other side of the river?" I asked.

"I was, but I got a better offer. My old editor at the Examiner retired. The new guy wanted me back and was willing to meet my requirements. Today is my second day."

"Nice raise and closer to home, huh? Congrats."

"Yes, I got a better salary and have final approval on any revisions to my stories. I guess you didn't notice my byline in the *County Examiner* this morning, then? I'm trying to get caught up on everything with the preacher's case."

"I'm sorry, Johnny. I didn't notice in the paper, but welcome back."

"I guess my name needs to be on the cover of the mystery novels you read to get your attention, Miss Love. Journalism is an unappreciated and thankless job."

"Okay, you've earned my sympathy as you intended. So, what do you want to know? Oh, and it's still Emma."

"I'd love to know anything you're willing to share, Emma. Are there any breakthroughs on the missing Preacher or leads on the murdered woman?"

"I think it's okay to tell you. I know the Sheriff's Office likes to keep the public informed unless it interferes with their case. Pastor Frank was found last night. He was floating on the Bay almost out to the Potomac."

"Floating? You mean like drowned and floating—dead?"

"Floating and dead, yes. The cause of death isn't determined yet, though. The body will be transported to Baltimore for that."

"Any idea how long he's been dead?"

"If you're asking for my unprofessional opinion, I won't even try to guess. It wouldn't serve any purpose, anyway."

"Are you sure, Emma? I could use a quote like that from, shall we say, an 'anonymous source close to the Sheriff's Department.'"

"Not happening, Johnny. Now, if you don't mind, I have a busy day ahead, but it was good to see you. Welcome back to Newtowne."

****

As I pulled into Cheryl's driveway, I spotted her huge black SUV sitting out front and parked my Bronco behind her. I smiled, wondering what the neighbors would say. I'm sure they'd wonder what my old jalopy's presence would do to their homes' real estate values.

Cheryl opened the door before I touched the doorbell. Her eyes were swollen, and her cheeks were damp with smudged rivulets of mascara. She rubbed her face with the sleeve of her pristine white robe, adding another black streak.

"Oh, Emma," she blurted. "Thank you for coming. Then you've heard. Of course, you've heard. Your Sam and—oh my, I'm such a mess. Please, come inside."

Cheryl's eyes swept the front yard and the street outside, then tightened the sash around her robe. She started to say something else, thought better of it, and hugged me instead. When she released me, and we turned back toward the door, a man now stood on the threshold. Dark-haired and perhaps six feet and an inch or so; his manner oozed refinement and, as so often comes with that trait, the taint of arrogance. He sniffed at the air as if it were of a lesser quality than he was accustomed to, or my deodorant had stopped working. His hand darted toward me as if wishing me to kiss his

114

ring. I took his soft hand in mine.

"Hello," he said. "I'm Gene Love, Cheryl's brother. What can we do for you?"

"Gene, she's your cousin, Uncle Dan's daughter Emma," Cheryl said. "You have been gone too long. Do you remember my brother, Emma?"

"I do, of course, but I couldn't have picked him out of a lineup. He was a few years older than I was when your folks still lived here. How long has it been?"

"Many years," Gene said and turned away. Cheryl scrunched up her nose.

"Excuse my brother, Emma. He is a man of few words," she said, "at least the spoken kind. I'm afraid he lost all social graces in the big city. To answer your question, I'd guess it's been ten years? I left for college a few years before you left Newtowne. Gene was still in high school. After I graduated, I married my Frank. I came home a few years after that when our father took ill. After Daddy passed, I was the one to stay, and I sent Gene to college. My little brother did all right for himself, too. He became a big-time reporter, though it's been years since we heard a word from him. Still, when Gene knew I was in trouble and needed him, he was here for me like magic. I didn't even need to ask."

"Perhaps we should step inside, ladies." Gene nodded across the street, where an elderly, blue-haired lady stood gawking at us while pretending to weed her flowers. "No need to give them more ammunition to gossip about."

Once inside, Cheryl rushed off to pour us a cup of coffee, and Gene escorted me into the sitting room. "I really must apologize, cousin. First, I apologize for not recognizing you, of course, but for the chilly reception, as well. Cheryl has had so much on her. She isn't handling it well emotionally. We've all been touched by grief."

Gene looked away from me toward the far corners of the ceiling.

"Yes, the hardest part of the human condition is loss. Poor Frank…"

"Yes, Frank, too. I must be here for Cheryl."

"I feel your loss might be more personal, Gene, and I'm sorry for yours. Was it recent?"

"Forgive me, Emma. I'm rather transparent, I'm afraid."

"There's no need to apologize. Was it someone close to you, then? If you don't mind my asking."

"Yes, my wife, and it was only a few months ago. That's why when Cheryl called…"

"Are you talking about me?" Cheryl asked, entering with three coffee cups on a tray. "He came last night after I called. And way faster than the speed limit would've allowed. It's a blessing Emma's boyfriend didn't catch you."

"That coffee smells wonderful, Sis."

"So, what did I miss? Not just talking about me, I hope?" Cheryl asked.

"Not at all. I apologized to Emma for being so rude to her. I am truly sorry, Emma, but you wouldn't believe the calls we've received or how often the doorbell has rung with people looking for the latest gossip and hoping to feed on someone else's misery."

"There are some like that, Gene. But some are just reaching out, so you know they're there if you need them. There's no book on how to help folks who are grieving. Nobody knows what to say or do. No words are good enough. Secretly, they thank whatever entity they believe in for sparing them the same tragedy. But most feel your pain and try to show that they care."

"I think you're a better person than I am, Miss Emma Love," Gene said.

Cheryl sipped coffee and choked back a sob. Gene jumped from his chair, sat beside her on the couch, and took her hand.

"I'm sorry, Sis. Let's change the subject."

"Where have you been living all these years, Gene?" I asked.

"After Newtowne and straight out of college, I was offered a good job in North Carolina. I've been there in one role or another ever since and made good money doing it. I'm considering moving back here with all that's happened in Cheryl's life and my own."

"That would be nice. I'm sure you'd be a comfort to each other."

"I'm feeling out my options, and we'll see how they pan out," Gene said.

I nodded and turned to Cheryl. "Do you remember those summers when we'd stay at Uncle Gene's cabin for a week? Fishing, swimming, and hiking in the woods, with no neighbors nearby. It was as close to heaven as you can get while still breathing."

"It was a simpler time." Gene smiled. "We didn't have a care in the world. Remember how cold the river was that one year when we went up in late spring?"

Cheryl's eyes wandered, perhaps traveling back in time.

"Do you still have the cabin?"

"I don't know. I guess it's still there." Gene looked at Cheryl, who shrugged her shoulders.

"I'll bet nobody has been there in years," Gene said. "If it hasn't collapsed, we could see if it is worth fixing up to sell when things settle down. Snakes and vermin probably took it over by now, though."

There was a pause in the conversation, and Cheryl shifted on her seat.

"Could I ask you a few questions, Cheryl? If you're up to it, I mean. I know you've had a horrible shock."

"Not as much of a shock as you might think. I had a terrible feeling about it all—about Frank, I mean. When you've been with someone for so long, you connect in a way where you can feel them. You know when they're close. You know when something's wrong. Frank wouldn't leave without a word, and when they found his car. Well, I knew there was a storm coming. I've been bracing myself for it…"

"Then maybe you are up to some questions?"

"I must think it was an accident, Emma. But if you're right and Frank was killed, will it help find out who did it to him? Is that what you're trying to do, Emma?"

"Yes, it is. Do you know of anyone who'd want to hurt Frank, Cheryl? Any old grudges that anyone had against him?"

"None that I can think of. Frank was a good man, a quiet man. He never did anyone any harm. He always wanted to help people. He was the first one knocking on your door to assist in trying times."

Gene cleared his throat and shook his head.

"I know, Gene. I know. Frank was—well, I have told you of my suspicions already, Emma. I can't see how that has any bearing on his accident."

"We can't assume it was an accident, Cheryl. The autopsy hasn't even started."

Gene stood up from the sofa. "It seems to me that would be the obvious conclusion, cousin. Number one, the man was a very poor swimmer. On the two occasions Frank and Cheryl visited us in North Carolina, he wouldn't even get in the pool. The most he would do was dip his toes at the edge. Frank would drown in a bathtub. Number two, he knew less about canoeing than I know about preaching, which isn't much. Why he'd attempt to paddle out in the bay is beyond me. I suspect it was a bucket list thing and part of his midlife crisis. Number three, he was a preacher, and everyone loved him. Why would anyone want to hurt Frank?"

"I don't know, Gene. That's what we're trying to find out," I said.

"Who's we? I've only seen you, Emma. What do the police think? Are they suspecting something different than an accidental death?"

"I can't speak for them, Gene, but there's been another mysterious death lately and…"

"Yes, I heard all about that too. Some young woman, probably a drug addict whom Frank may or may not know, overdoses on some experimental hallucinogenic plants, and they try to drag my sister into it. It's shameful how these small-town cops clutch at straws to harass their citizenry."

"Gene, that's enough," Cheryl said. "Sit back down."

"I'm here to support Cheryl," I said. "Also, I'm trying to ask questions, so the police do not have to be here asking them now."

"So, you are working with them."

"Yes, Gene. Cheryl knows that. Now, take a chill pill."

"Yes, please sit down. You make me nervous with all this hopping up and down," Cheryl said.

"Very well. I suppose I get a bit overprotective regarding my sister, Emma." He paused. "You do understand, I hope?"

I nodded and turned back to face Cheryl.

"Can I be blunt, Cheryl?"

"Of course you can, Emma. We're family, after all."

"You know you are one of the prime suspects in the death of the young woman, Marsha Johnson. It looks like Frank knew her. Did you? Have you seen her before, or have you ever seen the two of them together?"

"No. Well, I don't think so anyway. I didn't recognize the name, and the picture of her in the newspaper was grainy. The caption said it was several years old."

"They haven't released the cause of death to the public yet, Cheryl, but I can tell you this much. It was a poison from a plant that grows wild, a plant a botanist would be familiar with."

"Was it a berry or a root? There's jimsonweed, but it would take quite a bit of that, and it's not very palatable. Maybe deadly nightshade berries or water hemlock root? Hemlock is what killed Socrates, you know. I'd go with the nightshade berries if it were me, and I hoped they'd ingest it. I understand they're on the sweet side. Was it one of those?" Cheryl asked.

Gene dropped his head into his hands, and my

mouth opened wide enough to catch flies, as Nana Love says.

"Cheryl, please don't say anything like that to the police. Your knowledge of plants is another reason you're a suspect," I said.

"Nightshade is also called Belladonna, or beautiful woman in Italian. The Renaissance era ladies diluted it and used it to enlarge their pupils, which, one must suppose, the Renaissance men found titillating."

"Cheryl, really, don't..."

"Emma, everyone knows I love my plants. It's no secret. To hide that would be suspicious. Don't you agree? Besides, I can't count the number of people I've taught to differentiate between dangerous and edible plants. Some are not easy to tell apart. I showed the high school students for years. I've taught adults, too, who wanted to learn through the community college. Gene has attended one of those. Your friend Katrina Baker took the same class as your brother Daniel did a few years back."

"I guess you have a point there," I said.

"Everyone should try to get to know the world around them, Emma."

"You are right. I understand you still had a stockpile of wild herbs and berries in your storage shed. Were you planning to go back to teaching botany again?"

"I don't think so. I'm so busy with the flower shop these days that—Oh, I see what you did there. Yes, I had samples of many poisonous plants in the shed. They are mostly old specimens from my teaching days. And no, I didn't poison that girl with them."

"You told me you knew no one who hated Frank

enough to hurt him. Does that include you? You've confided in me about your suspicions about Frank's infidelity…"

"Oh, Emma, it's bad enough you think I'd harm that young woman. You don't think I'd kill Frank?" There was a catch in her voice, and her eyes welled up for the first time since I'd been there.

"No, I don't think you'd hurt Frank, but I have to ask."

"I'm sorry," she said and wiped her eyes with a tissue from the box on the end table beside her. "I didn't think I had any tears left in me."

Gene pulled a small trash can from under the table, and Cheryl tossed the tissue inside. The receptacle was about full.

"Do you need a break, Sis?" Gene asked. Cheryl shook her head, looked at me, and smiled.

"He is a darling little brother, isn't he, Emma? I swear he'd do anything for me."

I nodded and smiled back. "I'm glad he's here for you, Cheryl. But again, no, I do not think that you hurt Frank. I'm trying to ask you the same kinds of questions the cops will ask if Frank's death is determined to be a homicide. With Marsha Johnson's death, that is how the District Attorney will treat the case until there's proof otherwise. And you know the spouse is always the first suspect they look at."

"I appreciate that, Emma. I wouldn't have told you my suspicions about Frank's running around if I had plans to hurt him, though, would I? And I certainly wouldn't hurt some woman who was a total stranger to me."

We discussed the case some more—at least the

parts I was at liberty to disclose. I felt like I'd already dug in more than needed, but I did want Cheryl to be prepared. I thought some memory might shake out if it was just us talking. I said a silent prayer that Sam could delay the arrest warrant for Cheryl for a little longer...

Gene stood and offered his hand. I stood and shook it.

"It was nice to meet you again after all these years, Gene. Are you staying for a while?"

"Same here, Emma. I'm considering coming back home, as I mentioned. Do you think Newtowne will have me?"

"You said you are a writer for a living?"

"I'm a newspaper reporter. Journalism does have a bad reputation lately, and one that's not totally undeserved, but it's in my blood. I don't know how to do anything else."

I nodded at him and pulled Cheryl into my arms.

"I think it will all be cleared up soon, Cheryl. I'm so sorry for your loss. If there's anything I can do, you know how to get ahold of me. Both of you."

Gene walked me to the door, but before opening it, he stopped to straighten a shadow box containing white flowers with yellow stamens. I turned to Cheryl.

"That is lovely, Cheryl. What are they?" I asked.

"They are Easter lilies, of course," she answered. "We have them blooming everywhere in the spring. Half of the homes here have them in their yards. I'll dig some up for you if you'd like?"

Gene opened the front door for me, and it was graveyard quiet outside. No birds sang, no car sounds from the main road. It wasn't country quiet. I was used to that. It was a "storm is coming quiet," and a shiver ran down my back.

As the door closed behind me, tires squealed, entering the residential street. Police lights and sirens shattered the stillness.

Chapter Twelve

Two patrol cars stopped behind my Bronco, blocking my exit. Not that I was going anywhere before I found out what was happening. Sam exited the lead vehicle, wiped the sweat from his brow, and put on his deputy's hat. He held up a piece of paper and shook his head.

"Sam, tell me that's not Cheryl's arrest warrant?" I asked.

"Yeah, it is," Sam said. "Not my idea, but we didn't have much choice."

"What do you mean? Cheryl's just lost her husband. I already felt bad enough showing up here asking her all kinds of questions…"

"I know, Emma. We knew this was coming and I hoped it would be easier for her coming from you."

"Well, this isn't easier, Sam. Now you're going to arrest a grieving widow? I thought you would get the sheriff to hold off until things calmed down. What changed?"

"What changed is that we got multiple test results back from the lab this morning," Sam said and stared at me.

"What are you waiting for, Sam, a drumroll or for me to guess? What did the results say?"

"I didn't do this, Emma…I held off as long as I could."

"I know. Please, Sam."

"The results came back from the samples we'd taken in Katrina's shop and Cheryl's specimen jars. The tucked-away jelly bucket in the fridge at Katrina Baker's shop was poisoned with Belladonna," Sam said.

"How does that add up to Cheryl getting arrested?"

"We took Katrina in for questioning. I told her about Frank and she told us some things that implicated Cheryl. Also, the poisoned jelly filling had a spoon with Cheryl's fingerprints on it. We suspect she broke in to poison the jelly, knowing it was what her husband bought every morning."

"But did she?"

"Did she what? It's only circumstantial, maybe, but it is incriminating."

"I meant, did Cheryl know about Frank's particular donut purchases?"

Sam shrugged. "It looks that way."

"What did Kat tell you that put the spotlight on Cheryl? You know there's something there—some old grudge between the two of them. Cheryl gets riled up whenever Kat's name is mentioned."

"I could tell there was no love lost between them. I'd rather you talk to her and see if you get the same story or perhaps a little more. We released her, so she should be back at the bakery."

I nodded.

"I'm sorry, Emma. I must do this." As Sam climbed the steps to Cheryl's front door, his feet looked heavy, as if embedded in concrete. Before he rang the doorbell, the door flew open.

"What's the meaning of this, Deputy?" Gene

asked. "It isn't enough that you show up here to harass a widow in pain; you must do so with sirens blaring and lights blazing. Are you hoping to get your picture in the newspaper?" He pointed across the street. I turned to see Johnny Walker's "mini hearse" parked at the side of the road. The intrepid young reporter stood with his camera in hand. Gene waved him away, and oddly enough, Johnny shrugged his shoulders, got in his Halloween prop car, and drove away.

"I have a warrant for the arrest of Mrs. Cheryl Pratt. Will you please stand aside, sir?" Sam said.

Cheryl came to the door.

"Here I am, Sam. Let's get this over with. Gene, be a good brother and leave Sam be. He is just doing his job. Call my lawyer and tell him what's going on. Will you do that for me?"

"Of course," Gene replied.

Sam read Cheryl's rights but had the decency not to cuff her in front of all the neighbors. Many were standing behind their partially opened doors or peeking from the edge of their shadowed window blinds.

Cheryl smiled when they passed me on the way to Sam's cruiser.

"It's not your fault, Emma," she said. "Don't look so sad. This will all be straightened out soon. I didn't hurt that girl."

Sam's eyes looked moist, and I didn't think it was from the pollen. I said a silent prayer of thanks that I wasn't a cop.

****

The drive to Baker's Bakery took longer than usual. The traffic wasn't heavy, and it wasn't my sudden desire to obey the posted speed limits but a heavy heart that led to my light foot on the gas pedal. I stopped on the shoulder of the county road where it swung near Briton's Bay, sat in the Bronco, and stared at the water. I wished I were on my kayak, my cares floating away with the tides. But I had work to do.

The bakery was busy with the lunch crowd, and the customers were too busy for a real sit-down meal. They settled for a sweet instead. I decided to follow suit and got in line.

"Can I get a glazed donut and your strongest cup of coffee?" I asked when I made it to the front of the line. "Can we talk when things slow down, Kat?"

"That boyfriend of yours has me about talked out, Emma. He told me about Frank, although this being Newtowne, I'd already heard whispers. But sure, we can talk. It may be a bit," Katrina said.

I nodded, found a corner booth, and waited for the place to empty. Valerie came through the door behind the order counter and said something to Kat. Her eyes were bloodshot and swollen. I waved, but it didn't appear she noticed. She walked around the counter and headed for the front door. I stood up to follow her, but as I reached the door, she stepped into Newtowne's lone taxi, and they drove away.

I sat back down and waited. After what seemed to be hours, the bell over the door jingled as the last customer left the bakery. Katrina brought around the coffee pot, freshened my cup, and sat across from me.

"So, what can I do for you, Emma? Or should I ask—what questions did Sam forget to drill me on?"

"I don't know what Sam asked you, so I'll try not to be redundant."

"So, shoot. I have a lot of cleaning up to do."

"Okay. What caused the initial rift between you and Cheryl Pratt?"

"Ah, so it's like the old saying: blood is thicker than water, huh, my friend?" she asked, emphasizing the "friend" part.

"I am your friend, Kat. That's why I'd like to get to the bottom of this before anyone else is hurt."

"You asked about a rift? I think that implies we had some semblance of a relationship to begin with. There wasn't one. Cheryl never liked me, and I found her arrogance and hoity-toity ways repugnant."

"I'd heard that after high school, you were—"

"What do you know? You were long gone by then."

"What is with the attitude, Kat? I said I'd heard. Weren't the two of you close then?"

"That was a lifetime ago. And why were you questioning my Harper? Why are you dragging her into this?"

"I'm not. I spoke to all the girls on the volleyball team. I hoped they could shed some light on Frank Pratt's frame of mind."

"And about whether he'd been creeping out on Harper? You suspected that and didn't think to mention it to me—*friend?*"

"I didn't suspect it, Kat. There were rumors…"

"Ah, rumors…"

"You know how gossips are, Kat. When they see someone on a pedestal, they want to knock them down. That's truer with the clergy than anyone. Small-minded people want to drag them down to their level. In all his years here, there's never been a whisper of anything like that about Frank Pratt. So, no. I didn't, and I don't believe it. That said, would you have had me ignore the possibility? No matter how remote it was?"

Katrina didn't answer; she only shrugged her shoulders. Her face was still as red as a St. Merriam's County firetruck.

"I noticed Valerie leaving in a hurry. Is she okay?"

"I think so—just not feeling well. I hope it's not a bug. She and Sofia had a good weekend. Val needed some downtime. She was upset the other morning before they left for their shopping adventure."

"What was she upset over?"

"No idea. She didn't share. It's not like we are best friends and confidants, you know. When I came downstairs, she was teary-eyed and reading the paper at the dining room table. Maybe you should ask her if you need to know."

"Okay, I'll do that. So, back to you and Cheryl. What's the deal with the two of you?"

"I guess I might as well tell you what really happened before Cheryl tells you her distorted version of the truth."

"I'd love to hear it," I said.

"To make a long story short, I met Frank Pratt during the last semester of my senior year of high school. I was young, naïve, and had just gone through a breakup with Brian Nash; remember him? Our high school quarterback?"

"Yes, all the girls made moon eyes at him and envied you."

"They shouldn't have. He was easy on the eyes but way too full of himself and handsy. I wasn't ready for anything like that. So, he dumped me…"

"That's when you met Pastor Frank?"

"Yes, he was in his second year of college. It was before he transferred to the Seminary, and he was here on spring break with Cheryl. There was an attraction there—the older man thing, I guess. He seemed so worldly and sophisticated, at least, in my limited experience."

"You had a relationship with him, Kat?"

"I don't think I'd dignify what we had by calling it a relationship, especially with how it ended. It wasn't even an affair. It was one drunken night for both of us. The next day, he called me in tears. Said he had to see me. I met him, and he told me how sorry he was and that he felt he'd taken advantage of me. I suppose he did, given my age and inebriation, but I was eighteen and knew everything. I mentioned I was young and naive, but I wasn't a fool. I didn't hold it against him and told him so. Besides, I was old enough to know better."

"Was that the end of it? Did you think it was normal behavior for him?"

"No. He swore it was the last time, that he loved Cheryl and was turning over a new leaf in life. So, I gathered he'd enjoyed something of, shall we say, an active social life. It seemed to tear at him, though. I heard he quit drinking and entered the seminary shortly after."

"I'm guessing that Cheryl found out?"

"You didn't hear about it? No, I think you were gone by then. Yes, that conversation took place at Don's Burgers."

"The restaurant where this bakery is now?"

"Yes, almost pre-ordained, huh? As Frank was wiping the tears from his eyes, Cheryl stormed in. She did the best impression of a rabid dog I've ever seen. Yelling so loud it was incomprehensible. Of course, I was called every kind of loose woman, in gentile terms, but Cheryl's words weren't so reserved, and she wasn't holding back. I swear she was foaming at the mouth. When she was done with me or fresh out of curse words, she turned on Frank. His tongue lashing was less severe, but I knew her throat must be getting sore by then. When she dragged him out of the diner, you could've heard a pin drop or a mouse fart. If humiliating me was the objective, she was successful. I was the talk of the town for a while. Your mysterious disappearance became old news."

"Did you have any further contact with either of them after? Besides bakery sales, I mean?" I asked.

"Have you never visited Newtowne? Of course, I have. That's unavoidable in a small town like ours. Frank was never a problem. He still acts apologetic around me. Cheryl smiles with her fake smile to obscure the raving beast lurking beneath. But no altercations. I assume that's what you really wanted to know."

"One more thing, Kat?"

"Why not?"

"Did you ever mention to Cheryl what Frank's standing donut order was?"

"I told her about Frank meeting that woman outside, as I said before, but I didn't share what he ordered. Honestly, I'm worried that I only told her to hurt her. I hope I'm not that person. I want to think I told her because it was the right thing to do, but I can't help but question my motives. I don't think Frank was that kind of man anymore."

****

When I got home, I went straight to my laptop and pulled up "NeighborSnoop." I then searched for anything on Katrina and her daughter. Of particular interest was Harper's birth certificate. It showed Kat as the mother, and the father was listed as "Unknown."

Sam called then, and I answered on the second ring. "Hi, Sam. How's Cheryl doing?"

"She's doing great under the circumstances. They are still processing her; her brother and lawyer are already here. Did you get anything notable from Katrina?"

"Quite a bit. I assumed some from local gossip, but I'll fill you in tonight. I have a favor to ask."

"Anything that I can do."

"Can you run a DNA test?"

"Probably. If it's related to the case.".

"It is. I want you to run the two victims through DNA testing."

"Do you have a lead?"

"I'd rather not say yet. How long does it take to get the results?"

"It varies, but if we request a Rapid DNA Analysis, we should have it tomorrow or the next day at the latest."

Chapter Thirteen

Pulling into the driveway at home, I heard a small engine running in the backyard and walked around to investigate.

"Crab," I yelled over the noise of the garden tiller. "I didn't expect you today."

Crab, also known as Josh Grimes, was a young friend who was instrumental in finding my sister-in-law, Gwen, last year. He reached out to slow the machine until it idled.

"Hello, Miss Emma. After our bad storm, I thought I'd work the ground up for you. It might be too late for your corn, though."

"Well, thank you, sir. My garden loves it when you pay a visit. Me too. It appears you are about done, though. I haven't had a chance to chat with you in a while. Are you in a hurry to get home? I have pie in the fridge."

Crab wiped the sweat from his brow with his shirt sleeve. "Soon's I finish going down this row. Is that okay?"

"Head up to the house as soon as you finish then. I will grab us a soda and cut us each a big piece."

"Miss Love—I mean Emma?' I turned back toward him. "Is it that cherry pie like you had before?"

"Well, no, but it's blueberry."

"Even better. Blueberry's perfect."

As soon as the pie was cut and the iced glasses of soda poured, the tiller motor slowed, coughed a couple of times, and died. Moments later, Crab knocked at the door.

"Come on in," I shouted.

In his stocking feet and with soil-smudged cheeks, Crab reminded me of a young lad in a Dickens novel.

'Mind if I wash my hands, Miss?"

I pointed to the kitchen sink. When he was done, I sat at the table and asked him to join me.

"So, tell me what you've been up to? Are you, Eric the Red, and Pete the Sneak still hanging out? Staying out of mischief, I hope."

"Yes, ma'am, but folks don't call us that anymore—'cept you. I'm in middle school now, you know. I don't see them much. I only have that one class with Eric."

"I didn't know that. I'm sorry. So, it's Josh now, then?"

"No, ma'am. Crab is still fine, like I said, as long as it's you. And besides, Bryce is a new buddy. He's real smart and funny, too. You'd like him."

I suspected Crab's new, more formal address concerned the young ladies at Newtowne Middle School, but I didn't want to embarrass him with any questions.

"How is school going for you this year, Crab?"

"It's pretty good. Better'n last year for sure."

"Your mom said your grades were great last year. What went wrong?"

"Mom said I shouldn't say—with y'all being kin and all…"

"I know you were cutting the grass at my brother's

place. Did Daniel give you a hard time? Because if he did…"

"No, not your brother, Emma. Mr. Love treats me well, and Mrs. Love, she says I should call her Gwen, is so nice to me. She always has snacks, too. Last weekend, she brought me a huge stuffed ham sandwich for lunch. She puts a little extra red pepper in hers. Good stuff."

"So, what is better this year, then?"

"We had a substitute science teacher when Miss Carson had her baby. We ended up with Mrs. Pratt. Isn't she your cousin?"

"She is. Was she a hard grader?"

"She was for me. She gave me zeros on assignments she said I hadn't turned in. I'm glad I kept them because Dad took them to the parent-teacher conference. Pete's mom told Pete that Dad fussed at her something awful and that she better not hassle me just 'cause she had history with my mom. I don't know if they had other classes together or if it was just that one history class, but the next day, Mom looked on the 'puter, and my grades went way up. Sometimes, people with a lot of money aren't happy, so they treat people bad. That's what my dad told me. Why do they do that, Emma? They can get what they want, so they should be happier."

"I don't know, Crab, but your father sounds wise. I'm glad he got those grades straightened out with her, and I'm sorry my cousin was hard on you, but I'm not sure she's rich."

"Her brother must be then. He rented a boat from my dad's marina for the whole month. That isn't cheap. He must love going fishing."

I laughed at the thought of my city cousin fishing. "Maybe he wants to take his sister, Mrs. Pratt, out for some pleasure boating. It might put a smile back on her face."

"Mom says Mrs. Pratt was as two-faced as Janus. Whatever that means. I think it was because she'd smile at you just before she sent you to the principal's office. Mom said Mrs. Pratt would smile to your face while she stuck you with a knife. I never saw her with a knife, though."

"Janus was a two-headed Roman god, Crab. It's not a compliment."

"Two heads? I never heard of such a thing, Miss. Reckon those Romans didn't go to church much to learn anything about God, did they?"

"I guess not. Would you ask your mom to give me a call when she gets a chance, Crab? Or see if I could call on her one day soon?"

****

Crab left when his father's truck pulled into my driveway to collect him and the garden tiller. I went out with him and spoke briefly with Mr. Grimes. While Crab was out of earshot, I told him what a great kid he had. He seemed to know and smiled.

"Thank you, Miss Love. He thinks an awful lot of you as well," he said.

They waved as they pulled away. I grabbed my hoe and headed to the garden to check out Crab's labors. The freshly worked soil made hilling the soil around my tomatoes easier. The weeds were obliterated. Crab was a godsend.

My cell phone buzzed in my pocket. "Hello, Sam. Is Cheryl okay?"

"Honestly, Emma, I haven't been back to check on her in a while. It's crazy here today. In the middle of two murder investigations, there's not much time for the usual misbehaviors. I'm only calling to tell you I'm staying at my apartment tonight. It will be late before I can call it a day."

"That's fine, but if you are being honest, you probably need a break from me anyway." I laughed.

"Not at all. By the way, I submitted the request for a Rapid DNA Analysis."

"Thank you. I'll be very interested in the results."

"Me too, and I'm curious what relationship you hope we will find?"

"I think I'll go to Daniel and Gwen's tonight, Sam. I haven't seen Nana in a week. Hopefully, she will remember me."

"Oh, I see. You're going to get all mysterious on me, huh?"

"A woman has to have her secrets."

"Tell Daniel and Gwen I said hello and give Nana my regards, of course."

I thought that a night to myself would be a pleasant diversion from the stresses of the case and my love life. Sam had been hinting at us moving in together. I wasn't sure I was ready for that. I thought it was men who were supposed to be afraid of commitment. It wasn't that I didn't love him either. I guess I have loved him since we were high school sweethearts. I'm not sure I ever really got over him. He assures me he never got over me.

I'd spent all the years before returning to Newtowne caring for myself, not entirely by choice. I became a loner who depended on no one and that was enough. It had to be. Before Sam, everyone I ever leaned on folded up like a paper kite in a thunderstorm. I thought Sam was different—but was he? It took a long time before I even allowed myself to call him my boyfriend. Some scars run deep.

After a quick shower and change of clothes, I was soon driving up the lane to Love's Manor, Daniel and Gwen's residence. It was a half-mile driveway following the contour of old tobacco fields. Nowadays, soybeans or corn have replaced the noxious weed that once flourished here and established newfound Maryland as a prosperous colony. The farm and manor were my childhood home, and other than the crops grown there, not much had changed in the years I was away.

I slowed the Bronco as I passed the pond. The smell of honeysuckle flowers permeated the air, and an unexpected tear slid down my cheek. I couldn't help but think of Maya whenever I was near the pond that took her life.

"I miss you always, Maya," I whispered to my sister's unseen, but always felt, ghost. Many memories of Love's Manor were better off forgotten.

One of those memories involved my brother Daniel, who answered the door before I knocked a second time. Our old grudges were all but forgotten, but some scar tissue remained, camouflaging old wounds. Last year reminded us of what family meant when Gwen's life was in danger.

"Hey, Emma. What a nice surprise," he said. "Come in, please. Gwen will be delighted to see you."

"How about you, brother?"

"Of course." He wrapped me in his arms. "Nana

has also been asking about you."

"I'll head upstairs to have a chat then. If that is all right?"

"Of course. Don't be disappointed if she isn't very aware. It is so sad watching her forget—well, everything."

"Dementia is evil, brother."

The stairway walls were lined with portraits of family members, both living and those who'd passed beyond the veil. A newish picture of Daniel and Gwen was on display, and I wondered where and when they'd had it done. Next, in ascending order, were my parents. It must have been taken before Maya's death because they both smiled at the camera. That rarely happened after grief and alcohol took their toll on them, and us. Then there was Maya. She was sitting on Nana's lap, chewing on a strand of her own hair. Then another— Maya as a young teenager taken just before her death, looking just as I remembered her. I stared at her image, willing it to speak to me. But those moments only occurred when I slipped in or out of a deep sleep. I wiped my eyes and continued up the stairs. Nana would be sleeping soon.

"Come in, Emma," Nana responded to my knock.

"How did you know it was me?" I asked.

"Maya told me you'd be coming by today. As it was past lunch and well before dinner, I didn't expect it to be that brother of yours."

"He and Gwen take good care of you, don't they, Nana?"

"Of course, but I'm old and such a burden to them. I'm not much help these days."

"Nana, you could never be a burden to anyone."

Nana stared out the window, and I feared our conversation was over.

"What else did Maya have to say, Nana?"

"She is worried about you."

"What makes you say that?"

"What have you gotten yourself into, Emma? It may not end well if you don't pay attention. Let the chips fall where they may, or there will be consequences. More will die."

"Maya said all that?" I asked. It seemed I wasn't the only one in the family with hallucinations of Maya.

Nana's eyes clouded over, and her gaze drifted from me back to the window.

"Nana?"

"Well, hello, Sarah," she said. "What have you and my son been doing today? Did Maya miss the school bus again?"

"No, Nana, it's not Sarah. I'm her daughter, Emma. Remember?"

"Now, don't you worry about Emma, Sarah. You get Maya to school, and I'll watch her while you are gone."

I smiled at Nana, but my eyes blurred. I considered dementia the worst scourge known to man. Nana was always an articulate and educated woman. Where had my Nana gone? She dropped her head to her chest, and her eyes slid closed. I said goodbye and headed for the door. Nana mumbled something, and I walked back to her chair.

"What did you say, Nana?"

"Maya said she tries to talk to you, but you won't listen," she whispered with her eyes still closed..

A shiver ran up and down my spine.

****

I rushed down the steps, sparing not a moment to admire the family portraits, or to ponder my absence in any of them.. Gwen met me at the bottom of the stairs.

"How's my favorite sister-in-law and hero?" she asked. "Catching any bad guys?"

"Bad guys? No. Most days, I feel I'm no better than those internet scammers—shining light on affairs, prying into lives where I don't belong and harming only the innocent."

Gwen approached me, looked into my eyes, and wrapped me in a bear hug.

"Nope, not my Emma. But somebody needs a good stiff drink and some girl time."

"I really can't, Gwen, but thank you."

In true Gwen fashion, she would not take no for an answer. Though, I didn't fight all that hard. I thought what she suggested might be just what the doctor ordered. A few hours later, after enjoying two bottles of Daniel's homemade elderberry wine, I stood up to leave, but my vision swirled, and I sat back down. I wouldn't be driving home tonight.

Daniel came inside from his workshop and asked about dinner before noticing our "condition." His culinary talents were limited, but the sausage, egg, and cheese biscuits he prepared for us tasted like food fit for the gods. We inhaled it like buzzards on roadkill and with similar decorum.

Sometime after eating, I ended up in the bedroom at the end of the hallway, Mom and Dad's old room.

I woke to some real or imagined noise at three in the morning. I listened, but only the rustling of tree branches outside my window stirred on this windy night.

I wiped the sleep from my eyes, and Maya was there. Not as solid as in life, and her movements flowed with an unnatural grace.

"Okay," I said to myself, or my imagined apparition. "Nana says you wanted to talk. You have my undivided attention."

The corners of her mouth turned up in the beginning of a smile. One she usually reserved for private jokes between us—when she was alive.

"I thought I'd lost you," she said. "I think some of your old friends feel the same way."

"I know. This case has me searching all the dark cracks and crevices in Newtowne." I thought rather than spoke the words, but Maya nodded. "I must be missing something. Maybe a clue that flew over my head."

"Friends are always there to help. Who helped you before?"

"Besides you, you mean?"

"Besides me."

I blinked and reached for the glass of water on my nightstand. I turned back, and Maya was gone. I rolled over and, in minutes, fell asleep.

The sound of my cell phone vibrating woke me the second time.

"Hmm? 'Lo."

"Emma? Are you okay? You sound terrible."

'Good, Sam. Oh, well, no—hangover."

"I'm at your house. Where are you? I have coffee."

"I'm at Daniel's, but go on in. I'll get dressed and head over. Keep that coffee hot."

I placed a note on the dining room table before I

left.

Daniel, please get in touch with your lawyer. Cousin Cheryl might need his help. Her lawyer doesn't work capital cases. Love ya, Emma

Chapter Fourteen

The coffee was hot, and Sam had another pot started when I got home. Several cups would be needed to get me going on this day. He understood how I felt and perhaps why I'd felt the need for it. He spoke quietly, almost in a whisper.

"How's the family? Is Nana doing any better?"

"Better? No, she will never be better, Sam. It's all downhill from here for her."

Sam grabbed a napkin from the holder and wiped the corner of my eye.

"I know, Em. I'm sorry. I know how close you are."

"Let's not, Sam, but thank you." I stood and kissed his cheek. "You're a good man, hon."

"What are your plans for the day, Em? Maybe get some more sleep? That would be my suggestion."

"Abby doesn't have phone privileges, right? How about visitors?"

Daniel shrugged his shoulders. "You aren't thinking of…"

"Can you find out if I can see her today?"

His lips turned down at the edges, and he shifted his eyes away but nodded.

"Daniel's lawyer, Henry Stone, should be in to see Cheryl today. Did they set the bail hearing yet?" I asked.

"It might depend on how the district attorney charges her. If it's first-degree murder, she will get a hearing, but she is unlikely to get bail."

"I don't think Cheryl did it, Sam. I might have blinders on with her being my cousin, but in the worst case, any good lawyer should get the charge dropped to second-degree murder. If she did it, it was obviously a crime of passion, and we've found no definitive proof of premeditation."

"Dried berries used as the poison and placed in donuts? Appears premeditated. I'm hoping something else turns up too, Em, but for now, it's not looking good for Cheryl."

He slurped down his last sip of coffee, and I hugged him goodbye at the door.

****

I headed to town to pick up groceries and stop by the jail to check on Cheryl. Spending the night there couldn't have been pleasant for her.

When I pulled into the parking lot at the local grocery, my phone dinged with a text notification. It was from Daniel.

—*Got your note. Spoke with the lawyer this morning. He touched base with the courthouse. Cheryl's bail hearing is tomorrow at 9 a.m.*—

I texted back, —*Thank you, Daniel.*—

Daniel never passed up the opportunity to have the last word, and my phone jingled again.

—*I'll make sure Henry Stone sends her the bill.*—

The store was crowded, and as is the case in small towns everywhere, many known acquaintances slowed the shopping process. The produce was picked over. The brown bananas felt mushy, but the asparagus looked firm and fresh. The bread was day-old, but I threw a loaf in the cart anyway. I had a taste for a fried bologna sandwich like my dad used to make. It was one of Maya's favorites, too. We only got it when Mom wasn't home to fix what she called a "proper meal." It would be perfect for a quick lunch one day this week.

Food is one of my favorite forms of nostalgia—the tastes and the smells are a mouthful of memories.

I walked through the rest of the aisles but wasn't very impressed with or in enough need to add anything else to my cart. I made the mistake of passing the meat display near the deli counter. I decided to splurge on two freshly cut T-bone steaks. The thought of Sam working his magic on the grill made my mouth water.

As I loaded up the turnstile at the checkout, my cell rang. I glanced down to see an unfamiliar number. Telemarketers, perhaps, but I wouldn't take the chance.

"Hello, Emma Love speaking."

"Emma? It's Val. I heard you wanted to talk with me?"

"I would, Val, but now isn't a good time. I'm at the checkout at Murray's Market. Could we meet later? Maybe lunch?"

Val cleared her throat, and replied, "Sure, where and when is good for you?"

"How about noon at Sylvia's Diner?"

"High noon—that seems appropriate. I'll see you then."

****

Deputy Joyce was on desk duty at the jail and escorted me back to Cheryl's cell.

"I heard she had a hard night, Emma. Deputy Douglas said she was hollering in her sleep most of the night. I don't think she's accustomed to our deluxe accommodations."

"No, I'm sure she isn't, Joyce. She will have another night to adjust, if not more. The bail hearing is tomorrow."

"I'm sorry, Emma. I know she's your cousin, but good luck with that."

Cheryl looked like death warmed over. Her hair reminded me of a bird's nest if there ever was a bird so messy. Maybe a buzzard or cowbird would feel at home. Even a starling would demand a renovation. I couldn't see her face with her back turned toward me, and I hesitated to announce myself. From what Joyce said, she needed any sleep she could get. I turned back toward Joyce.

"Do you think—"

"Emma, thank the good Lord," Cheryl said, her voice hoarse and unsteady.

"I heard you had a rough night, Cuz. Are they treating you well?"

"I suppose as well as can be considering where I am and why I'm here."

"Sam said your bail hearing is tomorrow. Are you nervous?"

"Should I be? I didn't kill Frank or that young woman. An innocent person shouldn't have to be afraid, right?"

"I believe you, and I hope you are right about our justice system, but it might take a while to prove it," I answered.

"You'll figure it out, Emma. You always were a family person, and I never believed the things they used to say about you either."

I nearly smiled but chewed on the corners of my lip before it came to fruition. Cheryl had bad-mouthed me plenty, or so her fellow gossips said.

"Has Henry Stone been in to see you yet? Daniel says he is the best. Stone helped him out of a jam last year."

"Yes, he was here this morning. He thinks he can get me out on bail and that the evidence is strong but circumstantial. I told him it was circumstantial because I didn't kill anybody."

"That would be wonderful, Cheryl."

"He did say I might have to wear one of those ankle things—a monitor, he called it."

****

My next stop was Sylvia's Diner's parking lot. I sat in the Bronco to wait for Valerie, and she didn't make me wait long. The lone Newtowne taxi pulled up beside me. I felt terrible for forgetting that Val was a visitor here and had no wheels of her own.

She stepped out of the taxi and bent back inside to pay the driver. When she turned back toward me, her eyes were puffy and bloodshot. She smiled a smile that didn't reach her eyes and waved her fingers at me.

"Hi, Val. I hope you're hungry. I haven't eaten here yet, but I hear Sylvia lays out a nice spread."

"I'm not sure I can eat a thing, Emma. I don't have much appetite, but I've dreaded this conversation. We might as well get it over with."

I stared at her, wondering what revelations she might want to share that would bring on a case of nerves.

The hostess led us to a corner booth with a bay view. When she handed us the menus, we ordered our drinks.

"What do you recommend?" I asked.

"We have excellent crab cakes here. There's very little filler—just enough to hold it together, and it's all backfin meat," she suggested.

Val and I made idle chit-chat until our waitress arrived to take our order. I was surprised to see that I recognized her.

"Savannah, what are you doing here? Isn't today a school day?"

"Now, Miss Emma, you already wear a lot of hats—are you our new truant officer too?" She laughed.

"I must have my badge in here somewhere." I laughed, rummaging through my purse.

"That's okay. I'm on the work-study program at school, but we got off a half day today, anyway. The teachers are having in-service meetings. Besides, Martin is working on his dad's trotline. I work here mostly on weekends, and since Mrs. Pratt's troubles started, she asked me to shut down the florist shop for now."

"Oh, yes. Cheryl told me. Do you like working here?"

"I do. I get to meet a lot of people. Sylvia always feeds me well, too well if what the scales tell me is true. She lets me take home anything extra, too. Mom loves that part. The pay is good, and the tips are great. Hint. Hint. Wink. Wink."

"Got it," I said. "I think we will make it easy on you. Val and I both want the crab cake sandwich."

"Fries?"

"Please, and cocktail sauce for me, and tartar sauce for Valerie."

When she was out of earshot, Val spoke up.

"Kat said you wanted to ask me some questions, Emma. What is it you want to know?"

She sat stiffly in the booth with her shoulders pulled back. That was too often a tell for a lie or someone planning to tell one. I hoped I was wrong.

"I was wondering if you knew the deceased woman we discovered, Marsha Johnson?"

"I did, well, a little, anyway. We went out a couple of times, and then I ran into her on the bus when we came to town. I didn't get a good look at—the body— on our float that night. I had no idea it was her."

"I see. You must have struck up a fast friendship, then? You barely knew her and had her staying at your friend's sister's house?" I asked.

I stared at her, and she looked away quickly. She rubbed her hand across her mouth, then rubbed her neck before she answered.

"Maybe we were a little more than friends."

"Were you much more?"

"You're getting a bit too personal, Emma. You and I don't know each other that well."

"You are right, Val. I'm sorry."

She took a deep breath and sank back into the booth's cushions.

"It is more of a police matter. I was only trying to help." I stood up and excused myself to freshen up. Val's lips were tight. She didn't answer, only nodded.

In the ladies' room, I texted Sam.

—May have someone you need to question. I think she may know more than she is letting on.—

My phone dinged with Sam's reply.

—Let me know. Have an interesting development

too. Call when you can.—

I washed my hands, and Savannah walked in while I held them under the dryer.

"Hey, Emma. Is your friend okay? She looks like she just lost her best friend, or her puppy died."

"She's fine. Just getting something off her chest."

I glanced under the stall doors and saw we were alone in the bathroom.

"Savannah, can I ask you something?"

She shrugged her shoulders. "Sure, I guess."

"The other day when we spoke, you mentioned that Harper thought her mom was having an affair with Coach Frank. Did she tell you why she thought that?"

"I guess I shouldn't tell tales out of school, if you'll pardon the pun. Harper said she had seen them together over in Chapman County a few nights before. I don't know what all transpired, except Harper said it made her feel icky." Savannah looked away for a moment. "I'd rather not say anything else, Emma. It's kinda Harper's story to tell and all."

She raised her eyebrows, then flipped back her blonde curls.

"Thank you, Savannah, I appreciate it," I said and headed back to our booth.

Valerie was still there. She was tearing small pieces off her napkin and rolling them into tiny balls. She stopped and looked up as I sat back down.

"Are you okay?" I asked.

"I'm not feeling the best, but I suspect you already know that," she said.

"How so?"

"About Marsha and me. I guess you'd say we'd become more than casual friends. We were in a relationship. It was in the early stages. She wanted to come to Newtowne with me to meet my friends. She said she knew someone who lived nearby and hoped to meet up with them. At least, that is what she told me. I started to have doubts when she'd beg off something the three of us had planned to do together…"

"You, Sofia, and Marsha?"

"Yes. She skipped out on a movie we all wanted to see and then breakfast one morning. Sofia said she showed up outside the bakery with that man instead."

"You thought she did the same thing on our kayak trip?"

"Yes. But I didn't know what had happened. I still thought so when she didn't come back to join us on our shopping weekend—until I saw the paper that morning…"

"You recognized her?"

"It was blurry, but of course I did, and it ripped my heart in two. I'd been so jealous. I thought she'd met up with an old lover. I assumed that they'd spent the night together. Then, that picture of her was pale white like a ghost, and her face was so bloated. It was too much. Emma, I…"

"It's okay, Val. I understand." I put my hand over hers and nodded toward the walkway where Savannah approached with our food tray. I quickly handed her a napkin, and she dried her eyes.

"You ladies are going to love these. I told Sylvia you were special friends, and she doubled up on the crab meat. Enjoy," she said. She glanced at Val, then at me, and scurried away.

I did enjoy mine. Val, however, only picked at hers. Eventually, the color returned to her face, and the tears dried.

"Jealousy is a terrible thing, Val. I understand how you felt. Don't be too hard on yourself. The green-eyed monster can ruin any relationship."

"Guess I never realized I was the jealous type before."

"Love makes us do things," I said. "Things we didn't think we were capable of."

Valerie sniffed and wiped at her eyes with her napkin again. She pushed her uneaten food away from her.

"I think I've had enough, Emma, and can we maybe talk about something else?"

I nodded. "Of course. So, tell me, how do you like working at the bakery?"

"Huh?" She sat up as erect as a fashion model on the runway.

"Kat told me you'd been a great help to her behind the counter and that you have become quite a baker. She said your donuts were as good as hers, which is saying something."

"Oh," she answered. "I really don't feel very well, Emma."

"Maybe we should go, then."

Valerie waved Savannah down. "Could you bring us the check?"

She didn't wait for the check to come. Her face turned an unnatural green, and I thought she might lose what little bits of crab she'd eaten.

"Go," I said. "I've got this."

Val nodded and raced for the door, napkin in hand. Kneeling in the gravel parking lot, the sounds coming from her had the other diners turning the same color as

I'd seen on her face moments before. Someone must have texted the taxi that appeared with perfect timing. A small bottle was retrieved from her purse and she squirted some of its contents into her mouth. Wiping her lips with the napkin, she jumped inside and off they went.

****

The conversations with Valerie and Savannah gave me much to ponder and raised more questions than answers. I tried Sam's phone number, but it went to voicemail. I started to leave a detailed message, but I thought better of it and asked him to call me when he got a chance.

Pulling out of the parking lot, I decided to head toward the bakery. If Susannah were off from school, Harper would be as well. Perhaps I could get a moment alone with her if Katrina would allow it. For once, fate was on my side. Harper stepped out of the bakery, and I placed the Bronco's shifter in Park. I wound down the window and waved her over.

"Do you have a moment to talk, Harper?"

"Sure, Emma. Do you want to go inside? Mom has a fresh pot of coffee brewing."

"I'd rather it just be us for now. Would that be okay?"

She got a 'deer in the headlights' look in her eyes but nodded, walked around to the passenger's side, and climbed in. I took a deep breath. I felt dirty knowing what I was about to do, but I saw no other way to find out the next piece of the puzzle.

"So, what's up?" she asked as she settled in her seat.

"I heard from a little bird that maybe you thought

something was happening between your mom and Frank Pratt. Would you tell me why you think that?"

"Hmm, what did the little bird, AKA Savannah, tell you? I swore her to secrecy, you know."

"Don't blame her, Harper. I think I cornered her, and she didn't say much. She said that was for you to tell."

"Well, I'd say it's my mom's story to tell if she chooses to. Maybe you should ask her these questions. Aren't you friends?"

"I will, but I didn't want to bring what you said into it," I assured her. "I'd rather there not be any surprises for the investigation to discover. Kat *is* my friend."

"I'm sorry, Emma. You might mean well, but I can't do this."

"Are you sure, Harper? It might help Kat, too."

"And you're so eager to help?"

"Don't you want to help her too?"

Harper shook her head and narrowed her moistened eyes. "I said no, Emma. No hard feelings, I hope."

"Of course not. I understand, Harper."

She nodded and reached for the door handle.

"By the way...Kat tells me you have a new boyfriend. Is it serious?" I asked.

Harper's face flushed a medium shade of red. "Serious? No, I just turned fifteen, Emma."

"Nice guy, though? Good family?"

"His name is Kyle Burroughs," she said. "Maybe you should go pry into his life too. His family owns the hardware store, so I guess he is from the right side of the tracks, as you old folks say."

"Geez, Harper. I say that myself."

"You said it. I didn't, Emma." She drew her lips into a tight line. "Leave me and my mother alone, Emma," she said and slammed the car door.

Harper went back inside the bakery and spoke with Kat. I knew my name was Mud.

I leaned forward, with my forehead against the steering wheel in shame.

My phone rang, and I glanced at it. Sam. I started the Bronco.

"I'm sorry, Sam, but not now," I said.

"Are you okay?"

"I will be if we ever get to the bottom of this. Will I see you at my house?

"Yes, I may be late, but as soon as possible."

Chapter Fifteen

I drove slowly on the way back to my house. My vision kept blurring despite my best efforts to keep my eyes wiped dry.

I parked the Bronco and reached the front door before realizing I'd left my keys in the ignition. I retraced my steps and unlocked the door. The house was dark and offered no comfort. I tossed my keys onto the dining room table, then flung my purse onto the couch, its contents spilling across the floor.

Why had I asked Harper about her mother? Would she ever forgive me? Would Katrina? And should they? Did I deserve their forgiveness? What was the price of truth? Questions about myself and answers I didn't like but couldn't ignore rattled around in my brain. Finally, I crawled into my bed until a restless sleep salved my spirit.

My dreams were dark and dismal things, shrouded in a murky fog. They painted me in an unflattering light, and I struggled to wake. I watched myself as I transitioned from a green-skinned, pointy-hat-wearing witch, complete with a beak of a nose and the requisite obnoxious wart, to a greasy-haired torturer of the Inquisition. Poor Harper was stretched out on the rack while I tormented her about her loved ones. *I wasn't that bad...was I?*

Maya stepped in then. She placed her hand on my

cheek and smiled.

"You are always so hard on yourself, dear sister," she said. "Have you forgotten…?"

"I've forgotten nothing, Maya. I remember—too well. I only bring pain to the world, even to children."

"You bring justice, and peace, and love…"

"Are you and Sam comparing notes?" my dream me asked.

As Maya spoke in my mind, a parade of familiar faces drowned out her words. First, I saw Abby Dawson's husband, Michael, and their daughter, Jessie. "You gave us the peace and justice we deserved."

Daniel's wife, Gwen, favored me with a smile. "You saved my life," she said.

Then, I saw Pastor Frank and Marsha Johnson. They were hollow-eyed and pale. "We deserve peace, too," they said. "Our reputations are in tatters, and our lives are destroyed. All the good we did or would do is undone. Don't abandon us, Emma."

As they dissolved into the misty depths, Maya touched my cheek again. "And don't forget me."

"I'll never forget you, sister."

A door slammed, and my eyes flew open.

"Who were you talking to?"

Sam stood at the foot of my bed.

"No one," I said. "Just a bad dream."

"Maya?" he asked.

"Maya was there. She was the good part."

Sam sat on the bed beside me and brushed the hair back from my eyes. He said nothing at first. He was just there, and that was just what I needed. When I saw the shadows growing long outside the window, he stood up.

"I know it's been a hard day for you, my love.

Steaks on the grill might help. I'll get them going before it gets dark. Sound good?"

I nodded, and Sam rushed off to do his manly thing. Stand him before a stove, and you could count on burnt veggies or raw poultry. But plop a grill in front of him with an extra-long spatula in one hand and a meat fork in the other? Sam became a master chef. I mean, it is 'suck your fingers' and 'roll your eyes' good eating.

I must have dropped off again, as Sam was back at my side in what seemed like minutes.

"Ready to eat?" he asked.

"I am. Thank you, Sam. I'll go set the table."

"It's done. All that's needed at the table is you to make the meal complete."

We dug into the steaks as if we hadn't eaten in days. Sam cooked them just as I liked—still tender, juicy, and pink inside. I never understood the well-done aficionados. Why would anyone turn such a delicious piece of meat into a chewy, dry piece of cardboard? I mentioned as much to Sam.

"Ah, different strokes for different folks, I guess," he said.

"Tomorrow is Cheryl's bond hearing. Do you think there's any chance she'll be allowed bail?"

"I wondered how long it would be before you were back on the case. After your day, I hoped you'd take one night off."

"I don't think we can afford a night off. With the hearing tomorrow and we're no closer…"

"Okay, I'm with you. In answer to your question, I think she has a fair chance, or at least Henry Stone thinks she does, which is more important."

Sam forked another bite of T-bone into his mouth

160

and washed it down with a swallow of our local brewery's finest ale. He made a few orgasmic sounds as the tender morsel caressed his taste buds.

"So, what else happened today, Emma? Only if you are ready to talk about it, of course. If not, that's fine."

"Okay, but you go first. Your text mentioned an 'interesting new development,' I believe?"

"Yes, it did. Met an interesting young man today. He said he was Harper Baker's boyfriend and was the source of that information."

"You mean Kyle Burroughs?"

"You knew about him? How did…?"

"In my normal 'bull in a China shop' way. It's my modus operandi, as my criminal law professor would say. Digging and digging—no matter who is hurt. But how did your meeting with him come about?"

"Mrs. Grayson called about a prowler at her place last night. A deputy responded and caught Kyle creeping out of the woods near her place. I believe he had indulged in some adult beverages, and Deputy Douglas put him in a cell to sleep them off. I interviewed him before we released him. He said he lost his way in the woods after drinking a six-pack of beer that he snuck out of his dad's garage."

"Hopefully, he learned his lesson, but what bearing did that have on the case?" I asked.

"Well, during questioning, he said he was drinking because he had a big argument with his girlfriend, Harper. I was feeling sorry for the kid and asked what it was about. He said they went on a date to that new Italian restaurant in Chapman County. Well, the restaurant was the plan, anyway. He said they ended up at a burger joint. While they were waiting to be seated, Harper spotted her mom and Coach Frank at a table together. Kyle thought they acted like they were more than chummy."

I put my elbows on the table and my face in my hands. "Dear God," I heard my voice whisper.

"What's wrong?" Sam asked. "I thought that would make you happy. There's another suspect to add to the pool."

"It's not that, Sam. You did great. Me? Not so much. It cost me a friend and a piece of my soul for what you got for free."

"What do you mean?"

"It's a long, sad story that doesn't reflect well on yours truly. Maybe in a day or two. But while adding to our suspicions, I discovered Valerie has been helping Kat in the bakery, behind the counter, *and* making pastries. Believe me, Valerie is a jealous lover."

"Whose jealous lover? Frank Pratt?"

"No, the victim, Marsha Johnson."

"Really? Do you suspect her?"

"I guess I still suspect everyone. The evidence points to Cheryl or someone with a vendetta against her, at least, but it seems like everyone in that circle had motive and opportunity. We will need to do a lot of sorting out after the hearing tomorrow," I said.

"With adding a suspect, I think it is safe to say I've also eliminated one. Irene. I ran her prints against all we have related to this case, and there are no matches—not even a partial."

"Some good news, anyway, although we never really entertained her as a suspect," I said.

"Still, it gave me a warm fuzzy to eliminate her,"

Sam said. "By the way, I had your name put on Abigail Dawson's access list at the Sykesville Asylum today. I can't begin to say how much help you've been, but as to future access to the department? Sheriff Wathen is cracking down on that. He thinks there's been leaks in the case."

"How did our wonderful sheriff come to that conclusion?"

Sam reached out to one of the empty dining room chairs and lifted a copy of the local paper, *The County Examiner*.

"I don't know, but this article didn't help any," he said.

I unfolded it to the front page and read the headline:

"Wife of Murdered Community Leader Arrested" with a subheading reading:

"Pastor's Twisted Love Triangle?"

I read the entire article against my better judgment. Suzanne Abbot, the author of the hit piece, wrote about declining morals in St. Merriam's County. She laid into Cheryl as an entitled member of Newtowne society and cast shade on Pastor Frank's reputation at the same time.

She wrote, "How can we trust our community leaders? When you can't even trust your children's safety with this supposed man of the cloth? Or his demented lovers? What other perversions will be uncovered in this investigation? The answer is—only what they will tell us. Considering our sheriff's department, that won't be much. Not in that 'good old boy's network.' Who has forgotten the sheriff's brother and his legal problems? Have you forgotten the resulting slap on the wrist? I have not! Rest assured, good and faithful readers, *The County Examiner* and this reporter will be paying attention and will not be silenced."

There were a few more lines about the waste of the court's time holding a bail hearing the following day. "What judge would grant such a reprieve to a likely murderer? Only one in the defendant's pocket, that's who."

"Sorry, Sam," I said. "She wasted no love on Cheryl or the sheriff's department."

"Yes, even Judge Allen was cut with her razor-edged pen. Sheriff Wathen is afraid she will make the connection between you and Cheryl, which would taint our case."

"I'm acting as an unpaid private civilian, Sam. There's no conflict of interest with your department," I said.

"Just trying to avoid unnecessary criticism, Emma. You know how cases like this are tried first in the court of public opinion."

"Yes, I know it too well. So, low profile, I've got it."

"Emma Love, low profile? Yeah, I'm buying that." He laughed.

****

I didn't sleep great that night, but at least no strange dreams disturbed me. Sam couldn't have slept well either. It was his fault, though—every time his ice-cubed feet touched me, I shrieked. Nana used to say that cold hands meant a warm heart. She never mentioned feet, though. I'd have to ask her.

The sun's rays were starting to slither through the

pines at the bay's edge when I opened my eyes for the final time. The new day was dawning, and it promised to be a full one. I elbowed Sam in his ribs.

"Time to rise and shine, Deputy," I said in my best western outlaw's voice.

"Huh? What?" Sam was so eloquent in the mornings.

I pushed my index finger to his temple and made a clicking sound as I drew back my thumb. "Be still while I get up, or I'll make an opening in your head for your brains to leak out."

"Huh? Do you have a frog in your throat, Emma? You sound terrible."

"No, silly man. I was doing my Sam Spade impression."

"Hmm. Don't give up your day job, love." Yeah, Sam is both eloquent and imaginative in the mornings.

"Big day, and we are running late, baby," I said. "Toaster pastries may be our only breakfast option today."

"Coffee? Please tell me we have time for coffee," he said, looking at his watch.

"Maybe one here and one for the road."

Our showers were hurried, but the coffee was relaxed. Sam was dressed and ready when his phone alarm said it was time to go. He was required to be at the courthouse earlier than a mere spectator like me.

"I'll meet you there, Emma. Do you want to sneak in the back door like last time? I can have Deputy Joyce meet you if—"

"No, I'll go in the front door like everyone else. I don't expect newsmen there shoving microphones in my face like when Gwen was missing, and we went through this whole circus with Daniel."

"You sure? I'm betting it will be a clustered mess. Murder in a small town brings them out in droves. Who knows what a double murder with an implied sex scandal will bring."

"You think St. Merriam's County Office of Tourism paid for that hit piece in *The County Examiner*?" I laughed.

****

A circus wouldn't begin to describe the scene in front of the courthouse as even a circus has some semblance of order. There was none of that here. Two television crews waited like vultures on a wire for the courthouse doors to open. Their vans were parked on the lush lawn in front. The mayor would have a fit over that one. The county taxpayers would too, considering the cost of the sod last fall.

I pulled the Bronco into the side parking lot and walked toward the waiting mob. The sun was bright, with not a cloud in sight. I expected thunderclouds and rain to suit the day's theme, but the weather can surprise you as much as people can.

It was close to the time for the courthouse to open, and a line was forming at the door. Reporters weaved in and out through the queue, poking microphones in faces, hoping for a juicy quote for the five o'clock news. Some of our world-class gossips were questioned. A pair of blue-haired ladies broke ranks to get the opportunity to chat with them.

I picked out Valerie and Katrina in the crowd. Valerie waved, and Kat gave her the evil eye for doing so. I assumed Harper mentioned our chat. Cheryl's brother, Gene, was near the front of the line. He had a reporter with a County Examiner's hat on one side of him asking questions. Another with a WXPT microphone tugged on his suit jacket from the other side.

I'd no sooner noticed that when I felt a sharp tug on my shirt sleeve.

"Hello, Johnny Walker. It's good to see you," I said. "How's my favorite reporter? How come you're not up there pestering people?"

"I thought I'd pester you, Miss Love." He laughed. "Have you got a minute?"

"Are you still after an exclusive from the kidnapping/murder case from last year? And it's Emma, remember?"

"Yes, ma'am. But it was another thing…"

I didn't hear the rest of what he said. The courthouse doors swung open, and the crowd surged forward, pushing me along.

"I need to speak with you, Emma. First chance you get?"

I gave him the thumbs-up as the human tide swept me forward.

Chapter Sixteen

The entry requirement to access the courthouse "show" was navigating the two lines through a pair of metal detectors. It moved faster than I expected, but finding a spot to sit once inside was the next hurdle.

Cheryl caught my eye as I squeezed through and over a pair of seated gentlemen. They weren't gentlemanly enough to scoot over or stand to let me in, though. Cheryl gave me a quick wave of her fingers. I ignored it, pretending not to see. I didn't want to draw undue attention to myself with all the observant reporters in the room. Yup, low-key Emma, just like I promised Sam.

The judge entered the courtroom in her flowing black robe. The bailiff made his announcement, and we all stood.

"Who is that judge?" I asked the older man beside me. "I don't recognize her."

"I heard her name is Judge Barnes, and she's from up the road in Chapman County somewhere. She's said to be a tough one. I'll bet old Judge Allen didn't want the heat. He went on vacation to the Catskills."

The old man chuckled and took his seat when so instructed.

"Will the defendant please rise," the judge said. "Ladies and gentlemen, we are here today to hear the arguments for and against the defendant to determine the possibility of bail. That is our only purpose here, and I would remind the defense and prosecution of that fact. This is not a trial. Do you gentlemen have any questions regarding this?"

Both lawyers stood and shook their heads.

"No, Judge. We understand," they said in unison and reclaimed their seats.

Judge Barnes turned her attention back to Cheryl. "Mrs. Pratt, do you have anything to say in your defense prior to these two fine jurists oiling up their jaws?" she asked.

"No, ma'am—I mean, your honor. I will say I didn't hurt my husband, nor that hussy he was running around with."

"Mrs. Pratt..." the judge started.

"I've told them all that from the..."

"Mrs. Pratt, you aren't on trial here to..."

"I loved Frank. That woman led him astray..."

The courtroom gallery burst into laughter. Judge Barnes hammered down her gavel once, twice, three times, and silence returned. The tick-tock of the wall clock sounded ominous. The man beside me shifted in his seat, and I could hear his new shoes squeak.

"Order! I will have order in this courtroom!" the judge said. "Is that understood, Mrs. Pratt?"

"Yes, ma'am, but you said..."

"Mrs. Pratt! Sit down!"

"Yes, ma'am." Cheryl paled, nodded, and sat.

"Now, perhaps we can proceed in an orderly fashion. Mr. Gibson, would you like to begin for the state?"

There was motion on the opposite side of the courtroom, but I wasn't situated well enough to see. A tall, bone-thin man with receding black hair stood.

"Yes, your honor. I want to call the court's attention to the severity of the crime that this woman is charged with. The brutality of it. Mrs. Pratt, with malice aforethought, did murder…"

Henry Stone sprang to his feet, shaking his head. "Your Honor…"

"Please sit down, Mr. Stone," Judge Barnes said. "Mr. Gibson, I'm confident that you know better. Please comment on the issue at hand as it is related to this hearing. Don't force me to remind you again."

"Yes, your Honor," Gibson said. "As I have stated, this was a horrible crime, and I'll add that Mrs. Pratt is one of our most affluent residents. As such, her resources make her a flight risk. With her husband deceased and no other family to speak of, facing these charges, she is bound to flee the area. No bail should be considered, but no amount under a million dollars would force her to stay." Gibson sat back down, and the judge turned to his opponent.

"Mr. Stone, your turn," the judge said.

Henry Stone stood, adjusted his suit jacket, straightened his tie, and paced back and forth in front of the defendant's chair. He stopped midway between the judge's bench and Cheryl.

"Your Honor, my esteemed colleague has pointed out the reasons he feels should establish a ridiculous sum for bail. He has mentioned my client's financial standing in the community. In truth, her social standing is even higher than any financial considerations. She is a pillar of the community. No one has ever knocked on the Pratts' door in a time of need and been sent away. Yes, she pays her bills on time and doesn't need to worry about where her next meal will come from. That said, she is firmly middle class, not a Rockefeller."

A few giggles were heard in the court. The judge slapped her gavel once and eyed the audience. That was enough to silence the spectators.

Stone nodded toward the judge. "The evidence in this case is minimal, your honor. There is no 'smoking gun,' so to speak. As to being a flight risk, Mrs. Pratt's friends are here. Her home is here. In fact, her whole life is here. I'm sure she'd surrender her passport if it were the court's desire. She will meet any additional court expectations, as well. It would be a terrible injustice to hold this woman. I hope you will consider a reasonable bail amount."

"What do you consider reasonable, Mr. Stone?" Judge Barnes asked.

"We feel a hundred thousand, while punitive, would be appropriate. Thank you, your Honor." Henry Stone walked around to Cheryl and took his seat.

The judge slapped her gavel down twice and stood.

"Court will be in recess for fifteen minutes. Bailiff, please escort the prisoner to my chambers."

Cheryl looked at her attorney and whispered in his ear. Stone shook his head and shrugged his shoulders. He stood up to go with Cheryl, but the judge wasn't having it.

"We won't be needing you, Mr. Stone. Don't worry—we'll take good care of your client."

The bailiff took Cheryl's arm and followed the judge. The courtroom buzzed with heated conversations for the next fifteen minutes.

When the door they'd escaped through reopened, the courtroom went silent. The judge led the way, with

Cheryl following, escorted by the bailiff. When they all resumed their seats, the judge banged her gavel.

"Having interviewed the defendant and considering all the pertinent arguments presented here, I am setting bail at one hundred thousand dollars. The defendant will be required to wear an ankle monitor and be confined to her home. Are there any questions?"

Both lawyers shook their heads and responded, "No, your Honor."

"Mrs. Pratt, you are released to the St. Merriam's Sheriff's Department until the bail has been met and you are fitted with your monitor. Do you have any questions?"

"No, ma'am. Thank you."

"Please be aware that any violation of these terms will result in an immediate warrant for your arrest, and you will be held in custody until your trial. Do you understand?"

"Yes, ma'am."

The gavel slapped down three times, and the judge exited the courtroom.

****

I stayed in my seat as two deputies led Cheryl out the back door to the parking lot. I wasn't in as much of a hurry as the stampede that followed. When the crowd thinned, I felt a hand on my shoulder. Gene stood at my side. His eyes were wide open and unfocused.

"Gene? Are you alright?"

"I'm out of my depth, Emma. Do I need to find a bail bondsman, or are they court-appointed? Is there one in the tri-county area? What do they charge? Can they be trusted? I've heard such awful things about them."

"Slow down, Gene. Sadly, I do know a bit about the process. I'd be glad to help if you like?"

"Yes! Yes, I would. Thank you. Where do we start? I want her out of that horrid place as soon as possible."

"First, take a deep breath. Yes, we have a bail bondsman, and he's only a few blocks away. They generally charge ten percent of the total bail amount. Trustworthy? Well, Stanley Jones is a pervert. I wouldn't trust him to haul my trash, but a bondsman must be licensed. I doubt he'd sacrifice his business to cheat you."

"Would you go with me? When would you be able to go?"

"I will, and let's get started. By the time the bail is ironed out, the sheriff's office will have completed her paperwork and placed that damnable anklet."

****

Gene followed me down what the locals call "Louse Alley." I soon saw why by the state of repair of the businesses and the bedraggled old men with their brown-bagged refreshments in hand. The young, overdressed man loitering on the street corner was a cartoon cut-out cliché for a drug dealer. Fun times on Louse Alley.

I parked the Bronco in front of the old shop, which was marked with the sign 'Newtowne Bail and Pawn.' The pawn part was new since my last visit. Jones had expanded. Business must be booming. Otherwise, not much had changed since last year. The same dingy yellow, smoke-stained curtains were pulled tight over the windows, and layers of peeling paint adorned the door. Gene climbed out of his low-slung sports car. His upturned nose didn't hide his disdain.

"Fancy place," he said.

"Yeah, let's get it over with," I answered.

The inside of the bailsman's office didn't inspire confidence. The walls and ceiling panels were coated with the same residual smoke stains as the curtains. The room smelled of an overripe combination of stale cigar smoke, whiskey, and body odor, not necessarily in that order.

Jones sat at the same old flea-market-sale metal desk with his back to us, his phone attached to his ear. On the desk was a phone, a soup can full of pens (I couldn't discern the brand), and a nude, well-endowed mermaid figurine curled atop a large shell. The shell held a crushed half-smoked cigar butt. We sat in the two chairs with ripped upholstery in front of the desk. Jones hung up the phone and swiveled around to face us.

He was a late middle-aged man. His hair was jet-black, so black it could only come from a bottle for a man his age. My unkind thought was that it was from a can of black shoe polish. That would explain the greasiness. Jones was balding in front but combed his hair from the side and over to conceal it—a wasted effort. His face was pallid and reminded me of the vampires depicted in the teen movies, without the charm or good looks.

"Why, it's Miss Emma Love," he said, licking his lips. "How long has it been?"

Not long enough, I thought, but answered, "Close to a year, Mr. Jones. It seems you are doing well?"

"I am, but please, call me Stanley. As I recall, you prefer Miss Love?"

I nodded.

"Then this must be your young man, Major Mattingley?" He stood and extended his hand to Gene.

"No, this is my cousin, Gene Love," I answered. "We are here to obtain a bail guarantee for—"

"For Cheryl Love, I presume?"

"Exactly so," Gene replied.

"I believe the bail is one hundred thousand dollars. Is that correct?"

Gene nodded.

"For a surety bail in that amount, I'll require a non-refundable fee of ten thousand dollars from you."

"I'll write you a check," Gene said, retrieving his checkbook from an inside jacket pocket.

"What bank will the check be written against, Mr. Love?"

"It's a new account at the Newtowne Community Bank here in town," he answered.

The creepy dude picked up the landline from his desk and dialed a number. Stanley had it on speaker, and a woman's voice answered.

"Newtowne Community Bank, Evelyn speaking. Can I help you?"

"Good morning, Evelyn. This is Stanley from Newtowne Bail and Pawn."

"What do you need, Mr. Jones?" Evelyn asked, no longer sounding so cheery.

"I have a young man here, Mr. Gene Love, who requires my services. I want to verify funds to cover a ten-thousand-dollar check, please."

"One moment, please," she said, and the phone began playing elevator music.

Gene wrote out the check, and Evelyn's voice

returned.

"There are sufficient funds in the account, Mr. Jones."

"Thank you, Evelyn. I appreciate—"Jones began, but the line went dead.

"No courtesy these days," Jones muttered. "I assume Mrs. Pratt will be prepared to sign the documents showing her home as collateral?"

"She will," Gene answered.

"Well, then, Mr. Jones, Miss Jones, I'll get the funds to the sheriff's office as soon as possible. Thank you for using our service, especially you, Miss Love. I appreciate repeat customers, and the Love family is good for business."

I nodded, and we stood to leave.

"Perhaps you'd like to look around the pawnshop before you go?" Jones yelled as the door closed behind us.

In the parking lot, I called Sam. He answered on the first ring.

"Emma, hi. How did you and Gene make out? I saw you leaving together. I assume you went to the bail bondsman with him?"

"Yes, and we have all the paperwork done. The funds should be there soon, or so he promised."

"Did he at least pretend to be a human being this time, or does he need an impromptu visit?"

"All is good. I must wash my face and hands after being around him, though. That's all. How is Cheryl doing?"

"She's happy to get bail and should be. The judge gave her a big break. I think we were all surprised. She'll be ready to roll by the time Stanley Jones gets here. We should have time for lunch if you are interested?"

"I'd love that, but would it be okay if I brought Gene along? He looks so forlorn. He must really love his sister."

"Sure, why not? I've never met him, and maybe he'll share some insight into the young Emma Love."

"Are you calling me old, Major Deputy Samuel Mattingley?"

"Umm—a younger version of the young and very beautiful Emma Love? Oh, and it's Deputy Mattingley or Major Mattingley. We don't use them both together usually."

"Nice save, Deputy Dawg."

Chapter Seventeen

Sam chose the Newtowne Grill for lunch. My Bronco and Sam's cruiser pulled into the parking lot together. Several sets of eyes stared at us from the restaurant's windows. I got out of the Bronco and waved at them. They disappeared. I imagine they'd hoped to witness a drug bust or, at least, a speeding ticket. I almost felt sorry for the poor gossips. It would have been the highlight of their day, and they looked so disappointed.

I introduced the two men before we stepped inside. As usual with every restaurant in town, the waitresses immediately recognized Sam and escorted us to a corner booth.

"I have heard a lot about you, Sam," Gene said as he sat down. "It is good to put a face with the name."

"Same here, Gene. You can tell from the uniform what I do for a living. What about you?"

"Well, we met unofficially at Cheryl's house on the morning you arrested her, Deputy."

"Yes, I do remember. I am sorry. I hated doing that. It's part of my job, but it's hard when you feel sure it isn't the right person. But please, call me Sam."

"I think I'll stick with Deputy until this blows over. I'm sure you understand."

My jaw dropped!

"Gene, what is wrong with you? Sam has been in

Cheryl's corner since—"

"It's okay, Emma. I understand what Gene is saying. I'm not sure how I'd feel in a similar situation. If it were you, for instance."

"Thank you, Deputy. Maybe when this is done, we can move on. I plan to make Newtowne my home again. Cheryl will need me."

Our meal didn't improve from that point forward. Both men sat straight-backed and spoke only when spoken to. I tried to draw them both out, but my words were wasted on deaf ears. The food did not have the same flavor, and halfway through my sandwich, I stopped trying. When Gene waved down our server, I felt like I was the one granted bail.

He left enough money on the table to cover his meal and tip, thanked me for helping Cheryl, and left to wait for me in the Bronco.

"I'm sorry, Sam. That isn't the Gene I know or knew. I won't try to defend him for his rudeness, but he is very protective of his sister."

"Maybe too much. You'd think he wouldn't want to alienate anyone in law enforcement under the circumstances. I do understand, though, Emma. And I have plenty of experience with angry, cop-hating citizens. I won't shed any tears in my diary tonight."

"You have a diary?"

"Joking, Emma." He smiled for the first time today.

****

When I left the restaurant, I dropped Gene off at his sports car by the courthouse. We had little to say to each other. I was steamed over how he'd treated Sam, and he was lost in thoughts of his own. I stopped at my house to change clothes, then drove to Daniel's house, the local Love's Manor. Gwen met me walking up the sidewalk with a weeding hoe in one hand and dropped it to hug me.

"Hey, Emma. What brings you around? Mind you, I'm not complaining; it's great to see you."

"I should have called. I'm taking you away from your weeding. I hoped to visit Nana. Is that okay?"

"Of course it is. I'll join you shortly. I must wash up first, or Nana will lecture me about being presentable for my husband." She laughed.

Nana was perched by the window. It was also my favorite vantage point when it was my room many years ago.

"Good afternoon, Nana. How are you feeling today?"

"Hello, Gwen," she said.

"No, Nana, it's—"

"Maya, of course, it's you, sweet girl."

I shook my head and walked around to sit in the high-backed chair beside hers.

"Why, it's Emma. Why did you tell me you were Maya?" she asked. "You can't fool your old Nana, you know. But it isn't nice to play a trick on an old woman's vision either, child."

I smiled. "I'm sorry, Nana. I'm glad to see you are feeling so well, though."

"I feel as good as someone my age has a right to, Emma. Any better, and I'd have to pinch myself. I'd tell you not ever to get old, child, but the alternative is to die young. Then you'd miss so much of the good stuff."

"Tell me about the good stuff in the old days,

Nana. What was it like for you when you were young?"

"It was a good life, Sarah. We didn't get everything that we took a hankering to like the kids do nowadays, but we never lacked for nothing either. My pa had lived through hard times and rationing when he was small. It made him very careful with his money. My parents stored more food than we'd ever eat. I swear to Goshen, we lived in this great house surrounded by many acres of productive land, but you'd think my pa didn't have two pennies to rub together. But we always had plenty to eat."

I smiled with a heavy heart. I'd gone from my sister-in-law to my deceased sister to myself and now my mother. God, I hated dementia. "Great Grandpa sounds like a good father. I'll bet you loved him."

"Of course I did, child. He was my Pa. Even more, I respected and obeyed him—no matter what."

"Was he hard on you, Nana?"

"He made me listen like children should, but there was that one time."

"What happened, Nana?"

"What always happens between a father and his daughter? No boyfriend is ever good enough, and Billy Blake was no exception. Pa forbade me from ever seeing him again. It broke my heart. Billy recovered right, smart, fast though. He married that no-account Betty Wilson within the year. Everything might've been different if not for Abigail Dawson. Still, I never regretted marrying up with my Daniel. He was a good man."

"Abby Dawson? What did she have to do with it?" I asked.

"Child, that woman was the biggest snoop and

snitch in the tri-county area; never saw the likes of her. 'Course, she was just a child then, but she was still the same Abigail she is today."

"Abby does like to talk," I said.

"Doesn't care who she hurts either, Maya. I'll never forget that day. Billy and I was smooching in the barn, and that child had crossed our field where she didn't belong, and she spied us. She run up to the house and, straight off, told my pa. Out Pa comes with fire in his eyes and a shotgun on his shoulder. Threw a load of shot toward Billy's backside, he did. I don't know if he tried to hit him, but Pa was a good shot. After that, things weren't quite the same with me and Pa."

"I had no idea, Nana. I knew Abby was our number one gossip nowadays, but I guess she's made it a lifetime commitment."

"If anyone in St. Merriam's County has anything to hide or wants to keep private, Abigail Dawson will know all about it," Nana said.

Gwen joined us and witnessed Nana's alertness and, moments later, her apparent exhaustion. It was more than Nana had shared in quite a while. Her eyes grew heavy, and we left her to nap. As I closed the door behind us, I heard her voice as if talking in her sleep.

"Thank you, Emma. Come to see me again soon."

I was so happy to have had those special moments with her. It did my heart good. She also gave me a lot to think about. I'd nearly forgotten about Abby Dawson, but Nana put her back on my radar. I needed to call Sykesville to set up a visit with her soon.

First, though, it was a slow time at the bakery, and I might as well have that chat with Katrina. I hoped the knots in my stomach would uncoil by then.

****

Pulling up at the end of Love's Manor's long drive, I spotted Johnny Walker's mini-hearse-looking station wagon waiting on the side of the road. He ran toward me, waving a newspaper. He shoved it through my window.

"I didn't know, Emma. I need to talk to you," he said.

"I can't right now, Johnny, but I promise I'll do that interview soon."

I left him standing there; rude or not, I was on a mission.

"But Emma…" he shouted.

"Soon, Johnny. I promise," I yelled through the open window.

I glanced at the paper but couldn't see much, only *County Examiner Special Edition.*

I continued straight to Baker's Bakery and parked on the side, out of sight of the counter person. I thought Kat might disappear if she saw me coming or have her shotgun out.

Kat looked up when the bell jingled over her door.

"Hmm, what could you possibly want here, Miss Love?" she asked.

"I need to talk to you, Kat."

"Apologize to me, you mean?"

"Yes, that too."

"It better be a big crow with a side of humble pie. I think I have some in the oven," she said.

"I am sorry, Kat—so very sorry. Not so much for asking, but for doing so without you there, and worse, putting your sweet girl in an unconscionable position. There is no excuse for that. If it helps, I was sick to my stomach that night. I haven't forgiven myself, so I wouldn't expect you to. It's like an addiction, trying to get to the truth. I have a compulsion to turn over every rock. I hate myself for that part of myself and my job."

Kat gave me a half-smile. "That's a start anyway," she said. "As for your compulsion, well, you've always been a witch, but you have helped a lot of people. I'll give you that. Lose that, and you won't be Emma anymore. But if you pull any crap like that on me again…"

"I get it, and I won't. I hope Harper doesn't hate me forever."

"Harper is much more forgiving than I am."

"I do have some more questions, Kat."

"I'd expect no less. What is it that you are compelled to know?"

"I know you met Frank Pratt and had dinner at the new Italian restaurant in Chapman County. You said you had no more interaction with him, so why did you meet?"

"Did Harper tell you that? I was afraid she'd spotted us, but I only saw the back of her head."

"No, she didn't. Your daughter is so loyal to you; she never would. But you were seen."

"All right, Emma. I don't think this is any of your business because it has nothing to do with your murder case. Furthermore, if you tell Harper before I do, I will be your sworn enemy for the rest of your life. Are you still sure you want to know?"

"I do, and I'll keep it between us," I answered.

"I told you most of what happened in my senior year after the breakup with Brian Nash?" Kat asked.

I nodded.

"Then you know it was a stupid choice of a stupid, naïve me, so I'll lay my cards on the table. I knew what I was getting into, but I needed to feel loved, even for a weekend, after Brian dumped me. After, I discovered Frank had a girlfriend. He claimed he loved her and that he had a compulsion, not unlike you. He cried to me, Emma. He said he was an awful sinner and hoped God could forgive him. I knew Frank had enjoyed an active social life before that weekend. I didn't think I was the first, but after his confession, I was convinced I was the last. He called it a sickness. And maybe it was, but I believed he planned to turn his life around. Call me gullible, but—good Lord—he entered seminary after that, Emma!"

"What happened after that, Kat? There must be more to the story for it to resurface all these years later."

Katrina made a motion of zipping her lips, and pointed at mine. I nodded my understanding.

"Pastor Frank Pratt is Harper's father, Emma."

I thought my jaw would hit the table. Kat stood up, wiped her eyes, and stepped behind the counter. She returned with two cups and a pot of coffee.

"I don't know about you, but I need some of this," she said.

"My God, what did you do when you found out you were expecting?"

"I researched Frank. I was able to find out he had entered the seminary down there. Then I went up for a visit."

"How did you get your folks to go along with that? Did they know?"

"Not then, but obviously, they found out later. I

used you to get up there. I told them I'd heard from you. I said your address was on the note you sent, and I wanted to go and try to bring you home. My parents thought you walked on water and were some goody-two-shoes, so reluctantly, they agreed."

"Glad I could help. What did Frank say when you confronted him?" I asked.

"I didn't. I watched him, followed him home in the evenings, and spoke to some of his contemporaries—especially the girls, and everyone told the same story. Frank Pratt was the ever-faithful boyfriend, God-fearing and righteous. I couldn't do it. I was a willing participant, and I had options. Every day, I thank the Lord for holding my hand when I decided to keep Harper. She is the light in my life."

"Frank never knew?"

"That is why I met him at the Italian joint. That is when I told him. He said he wanted to meet Harper, but I wasn't ready for that to happen. I told him I'd have to think about it. When we left the restaurant, he pleaded some more to meet Harper. Then he said something weird. Maybe it came from the Bible in his jacket pocket. He said, 'The sins of my youth are coming home, my seed scattered to the winds, and I pray I can make reparations.' I think Frank was a decent man, Emma. Given all the good he has done, I think I did the right thing. Cheryl, too, though I hate to admit that. I don't believe the stories about Frank cheating on her, even if I told her what I saw. I guess we can all be a witch sometimes."

****

Home was my next stop, and Sam was already there. As it was early for him, perhaps his day improved after court and Gene's boring behavior at the restaurant. Looking at my phone revealed no calls or texts from him since then, and I felt like a poor excuse for a girlfriend. Gene's attitude cut him deeply, even if Sam would never admit it.

Retrieving the pile of bills and junk advertisements from the mailbox, I parked my Bronco beside his cruiser. Before closing the door, Johnny Walker's newspaper caught my eye and it and the mail were tossed onto the dining room table.

"Sam, where are you?"

"In the kitchen," he answered.

"Please, not hot dog casserole again."

"Have a seat and relax, Emma. I know it's been a long day for you."

"No worse than yours, I suppose," I said

"Oh, didn't you talk to Katrina then?"

"Well, there was that, though it went better than I expected."

I glanced at the mail, and there were no surprises. Then, I snapped open the "special edition" of the *County Examiner* to read the story written by the same Suzanne Abbot:

"Suspected Murderer Released on Bail!

"Today's court proceedings mark another travesty of justice by the St. Merriam's County court system. In an unprecedented ruling, Judge Lindsey Allen released a suspected dual murderer and probable sexual deviant back onto our streets! Judge Allen is well-known in our neighboring county for her leniency to criminals. This has been especially notable in cases where the defendant is female. Is this a worst-case scenario of sexism? Or has our illustrious and elitist Love family crossed her palms with silver?

"While bail is not entirely unheard of in a Second-Degree murder charge (which raises the question—why not First-Degree?), this reporter, in all her years following court cases, has never reviewed a case where bail on any murder charge was set at less than a quarter million dollars. But one hundred thousand? That is hardly punitive for a family whose worth is estimated in the millions! Some will say, 'But she has to wear an ankle monitor,' to which I say, big deal! Is it cast in stainless steel? What stops this crazed murderer from cutting it off and turning our streets into rivers of blood? The threat of incarceration? Hardly, as she is going there soon enough anyway—unless Chapman County's Judge Allen is sitting on the bench!

"So, I ask you, faithful readers—do you feel that justice was served? Will you feel safer in your beds tonight knowing such a wanton and murderous woman is on the prowl in our neighborhoods? What part of public safety does this judge not get as she returns to her plush waterfront home in Chapman County with St. Merriam's County and Cheryl Love Pratt in her rearview mirror?

"Today's court farce was not a trial, only a bail hearing, but there are ample facts available to the public:

—Pastor Frank Pratt betrayed his wife and our trust

—Cheryl Pratt knew of his indiscretion with a woman young enough to be his daughter

—Pastor Frank and his mistress were found murdered days apart

—The cause of death—poison belladonna berries in pastries

—The search warrant for Cheryl Pratt's home revealed Belladonna on-site

—Cheryl Pratt's fingerprints on a jelly spoon in the bakery

—Said jelly contained harmful levels of Belladonna poison and is the probable source

"Lawyers might try to convince you that this is all circumstantial, but it is damning in this reporter's eyes. The adage 'Where there is smoke, there is fire' springs to mind.

"As for me, my doors and windows will be locked tonight. I will huddle under my blankets, quivering at every sound in the darkness. I expect many sleepless nights until this travesty of justice is corrected. I suggest you do the same."

****

As I read the last of it, Sam came to the table with a platter of oven-fried chicken breasts. Though he'd spiced them perfectly, they were somewhat overcooked—not that I'd ever tell Sam that. After all, his grill wasn't involved.

I handed him the paper, and he began to eat as he read.

"Johnny Walker said they have a new editor at the paper. I can't believe he allowed this story to go to print. It's libelous, and the reporter has an ax to grind against poor Cheryl. She's already convicted her. I hope Cheryl doesn't see it."

"She will have a case to sue for slander, but *after* the trial is over. Public opinion will be sour enough after this," Sam said.

"Maybe Gene knows someone who can help rein them in. As a journalist, he may have some contacts."

After dinner, I cleared the table, and Sam offered to help.

"Nah, you've had a miserable day too. Relax. I won't be a minute."

He hugged me, lifted me off my feet, and kissed me.

"I love you, Emma Love," he whispered in my ear. "We will get through this."

Nothing says 'I love you' like a night of cuddling.

Chapter Eighteen

The following day, my first order of business (well after my second cup of coffee) was to call Sykesville Asylum and make an appointment to visit with Abby Dawson. It was a long shot, but I've followed up on less. I'd long ago learned not to take any suggestions from Nana lightly. Or dismissed any dream sequences from Maya, for that matter. My sister never steered me wrong—not in this life or the next, and I'd take clues in any way I could get them.

A trip to Sykesville Asylum meant a thirty-minute drive, and my appointment with Abby was forty minutes away. With my coffee cup rinsed out and in the sink, I texted Sam. —I'm on my way— and then climbed into the Bronco.

Traveling on the Interstate was unnecessary, so it was a pleasant drive. In fact, the scenery crisscrossing our rivers and streams was spectacular. The redbud trees were in full bloom, and pink and scarlet red crepe myrtles lined the driveways of the rare houses I passed. My cell phone rang when I turned down the county road leading to my destination. A glance revealed the call was from Sam.

"Hey, Sam. What's up?"

"You aren't driving, are you?"

"No, Deputy Mattingley, I am not. I'm on the last leg into the asylum and pulled over on the shoulder when I saw it was you. I've done the speed limit here and have my seat belt on, too. Shall I send you a pic?"

"No, ma'am, I'll take your word for it this time." He laughed.

"What's up?"

"Remember that DNA sample you wanted on Frank Pratt and Marsha Johnson?"

"Of course…"

"We got the test results back, and it's a good thing you are sitting down. They show that Frank Pratt and Marsha Johnson had a 50% DNA match. That means they were either father and daughter or siblings. And given the age differential…"

"Dear God, there were two of them."

"Huh? Two of what? What do you mean?" Sam asked.

"Sorry, I was thinking out loud. Never mind."

"I think and hope that means 'I'll tell you about it later.'"

"I will, but I'm sworn to secrecy for the moment."

"Do I need to know? Is it case-related?" he asked.

"I hope not; it's just idle gossip at this point."

Sam trusted my instincts and let it go at that. We said our goodbyes, and I dropped the shifter into drive. My mind sorted through the new information.

Frank told Kat his sin was the seeds he'd scattered in the wind. Irene said Frank had discovered things that would destroy his marriage if they came to light. Those 'some things' could only be Marsha Johnson and Harper Baker! This did not help Cheryl. Frank's admissions might grease her slide to "Old Sparky," the chair of two thousand volts.

****

I checked in with the receptionist in Sykesville's foyer. I passed her my driver's license, and she compared it to my name on the sign-in log. Then she looked from it to my face, finally satisfied that I was who I said I was and not trying to break out any of the "guests."

An orderly escorted me to Abby's room, and I knocked on the door.

"Come on in. It's not like there's any privacy in this joint anyway," Abby answered.

"Good morning. How are they treating you, Abby?" I asked.

"Well, if it's not my favorite neighbor. I'm fine, child. Three meals a day, and I don't have to cook a single one. I do miss my boy, though, but how are you doing, Emma?"

"I'm good. Keeping busy."

"And that handsome young boyfriend, the deputy? How is he shaping up? Is he a keeper?"

"Time will tell, but it's looking good for him so far." I laughed.

"A little birdy told me that some folks have been out at my house, doing some painting and such. Your doings, I suppose?"

"Daniel and I might have helped that along a bit. We thought it would be nice for Jack once he turns eighteen and is out on his own."

"That is neighborly of you. Please thank Daniel for me. too. 'Course y'all are why his momma is in this place, and he is in that home."

"Abby, I'm sorry about how—"

"Now don't you fret, Emma. You know I'm joshing you. You did what you thought best and always did.

That's about the best a body can do, and it will all turn out. But tell me, what brings you here to see your old friend, Abby? Unless I miss my guess, some case has got you all worked up."

"I did want to see you, Abby. It's been too long, but as you know, there will always be a case."

"You still looking for Mrs. Abell's cat? Misty, I believe she named it. She should've called it Zebra with those black and white stripes."

"No, ma'am, this case is a bit more serious…"

"More serious than someone's missing pet?"

"No, ma'am, I mean—well, there's a murder involved." I bit my lip, embarrassed by how easily she'd frustrated me.

"Now, I heard there were two murders. Is that the same case? You're wanting to know about that reverend fellow from the rich people's church and the woman he was seeing?"

"Yes, I was wondering if you knew anything that might be related in any way."

"I know the good preacher might be somebody's daddy that he oughtn't to be."

"How did you—umm, is there anything else you want to share?" I asked.

"Well, if you're asking my opinion. I never did like that cousin of yours, but I don't reckon Cheryl Pratt did the deed. She is two-faced, vindictive, and far too uppity for her upbringing, but she doesn't have the gumption. You know me, Emma; what you see is what you get."

"Were there problems in their home? I never heard anything when I was growing up."

"You were a child, Emma. Parents don't share such

things with their children, and I always kept my ear to the ground and doorways, too. You can learn a lot that way."

"Do you know what happened, Abby?"

"I can't say. I never saw anything with my own eyes, and I'm not one for idle gossip."

Nearly choking on a sip of water, I replied, "I understand, but what was the rumor?"

Abby turned her head to one side, her eyes narrowing to slits.

"It sure has been nice having you here for a visit, neighbor. You'll watch out for my boy, won't you? Jack's a good boy. He just needs a gentle shove in the way of the Lord once in a while."

I nodded and bent down to hug her before I took my leave.

"I miss you, Abby, and I hope you're back home soon."

As I reached for the door handle, Abby cleared her throat.

"You know you've always been one of my favorites, Emma. Do you remember that young fellow you befriended last year? He called himself 'Crab' or some such?"

"Yes, ma'am, his real name is Josh Grimes."

"That's the one. You might ask his mother some of those questions. She's about Cheryl Pratt's age and likes to talk."

I left there amazed at how much Abby kept up with and wondering about her sources. Even while incarcerated miles away in Sykesville, she had her finger on the pulse of Newtowne. It was uncanny. I wondered if she had her own 'Maya' to tell her things in her sleep.

****

The drive home was pleasantly uneventful, and I appreciated the lack of drama. I stopped for lunch at a small diner halfway home and called Sam.

"Hey, love," I said when he answered.

"Hi, Em. How did everything go with Abby? Good visit? Learn anything new?"

"Not really, unless you count that the woman must be clairvoyant. I swear she hasn't missed a trick since she's been in there, not that she ever did. She gave me a lead or someone to talk to about a possible lead, though."

"Who is that?" he asked.

"Crab Grimes' mother, Cathy. Abby thinks she might know some things about the family that aren't public knowledge."

"So, all roads lead back to Cheryl? It seems so at the sheriff's department, too. Deputy Joyce told me there's been no investigation into anyone else since Cheryl was arrested. I asked Joyce to follow up on something this morning, and she told me. Sheriff Wathen considers the Pratt/Johnson murder case solved. I guess I'm the only one who still has questions and the last to know."

"My take is Wathen didn't want you to have the resources to show him up—again."

"Maybe so, but maybe he wants to go out with no murder cases still open."

"Well, I guess I'm it, then—wait, what do you mean by going out? Where is he going?" I asked.

"Sheriff Wathen isn't running for reelection. A town in Western Maryland offered him a position he said he couldn't refuse."

"So that means—oh, Sam, you'll make a wonderful sheriff."

"Don't count our chickens before they're hatched, Emma. Besides, it will be some time next Spring before his new position opens."

"I can't help it, Sam. I'm so excited for you."

"Maybe if I was the Big Cheese, we could finally become roomies."

"Ha-ha, now, don't get ahead of yourself, Deputy. Did you forget what you just said about enumerating poultry?"

Sam laughed. "No. I didn't forget. What are you getting into after lunch?"

"I'm driving straight home. I think I have a kayaking customer at two o'clock."

"You think you do? Did Abby gaze into her crystal ball and see someone pulling into your driveway?"

"No, something a tad more mundane than that. I silenced my phone while I chatted with Abby, and the reception there was horrible. I got a voicemail but couldn't make out much of it. A lady said if I got her message and was home at two, she'd like to try kayaking. I'll try to call her back when we disconnect. The reception is better here in the diner."

"I'll leave you to it, then. If you do go out, please text me," Sam said.

I scrolled down to my voicemails and hit the phone icon to call my prospective kayaker. My call went to her voicemail, and the robotic voice informed me that her mailbox was full.

I texted Sam.—*Kayaking doesn't look promising. My call went unanswered.*—

****

When I got home, I changed into more appropriate attire for the river: cut-off shorts, a halter top, and water shoes. I knew the water was still cool, but the sun was merciless these afternoons. When it reflected off the water back at me, it was a double whammy. Once I added the vest-style life preserver, I'd be too warm.

Outside, I pulled a pair of bright yellow kayaks from the rack in case the woman showed up. I added two paddles and whistles and packed four water bottles in my tiny cooler. My cellphone's alarm rang to advise me it was 1:45. I had time for a short break, and the porch swing was calling my name. As soon as I settled back with the mystery novel I'd been reading, I heard the crunch of tires on gravel and went down to greet my client.

The car looked familiar, but I couldn't see the driver through the sun's reflection off the car's tinted glass.

"Hi, Emma. Do you remember me?" she asked in a voice as familiar as the car was, but I could not place either one. Then she stepped out. It was like the hands of fate were perched on my shoulder—or perhaps Abby did have a crystal ball.

"Well, Cathy Grimes, I'm delighted to see you," I said.

"Josh said you needed to speak with me about something. I'm sorry I haven't had a chance to get back to you before now."

"Oh, that's no problem, Cathy. Your timing couldn't be better, in fact. Was it you who called about kayaking? I had a terrible connection and couldn't determine who it was."

"It was. I knew you wanted to chat, and I had some free time with all my little people in school. And I always wanted to try kayaking, so…"

"Say no more," I said. "That's a splendid idea. We can chat and paddle to our heart's content. How much time do you have?"

She pulled her cell from her pocket and frowned. "Not as much as I'd like. Josh is staying after school for basketball practice, and I must pick him up at four-thirty. He's in middle school now, you know."

"If it's your first time, Cathy, that will be long enough. Not that you aren't in good shape, but paddling uses different muscles. Should we go get our paddles wet?"

Before we climbed into our crafts, I texted Sam. — *My kayaking client came—Cathy Grimes. I hope to see you for dinner!*—

The bay was smooth as glass, a perfect time to take out a first-time kayaker. Cathy quickly mastered the strokes as we did circles, stops, and abrupt turns in the deep pool in front of my dock. When she was comfortable with her newfound skills, we ventured further out. The water was slightly choppy there, but we could maintain our pace while paddling alongside each other.

"Emma, I confess to a degree of curiosity. What did you want to talk to me about? Josh hasn't been a nuisance to you, has he?"

"Not at all. I love it when he comes for a visit. He is so generous in spirit and smart, too. He's always thinking and puzzling people out."

"I hope you're being honest. I know that Joshua can be a handful, and I've told him not to show up at people's doors uninvited. But when he likes you, he shows little restraint and wears his heart on his sleeve. I'm always on the lookout for that first pony-tailed crush who will break his heart."

"That would be one foolish girl child, Cathy, and he can read a person quite well for his age."

She nodded and paused, holding her paddle across the gunwales of the kayak.

"Now my curiosity is really triggered. If not, Josh, what did you want to ask me about?"

"Josh said you had some strong opinions about Cheryl Pratt, and—"

"I'm sorry, Emma. He shouldn't have said that. Sometimes my mouth gets me in trouble, and I must always be on my guard with little ears listening to every word—especially with the words you wish you could call back," she said.

"Someone else told me you might know something about the family. Something that may have happened when Gene and Cheryl were young? I hate to put you on the spot, and I'm not asking for scandal or gossip. I think you may know something that might help the case. If it isn't, my lips are sealed."

"I'm sure it doesn't, Emma. It was a very long time ago. When they were youngsters, Gene and Cheryl had a hard life. You wouldn't think so. They had a lovely home. From all reports, Gene Senior had a good job and made a small fortune on the stock market. Gene Junior and Cheryl went to the best private schools. I know because Cheryl and I were best friends back then. But at home, it was as if they didn't exist. Neither parent paid any attention to them. They had to prepare their own dinners—when there was food available to make.

The elder Loves were more concerned with their next bottle than they were with their children. That made Gene and Cheryl as close as any two siblings I've known.

"Cheryl was a couple of years older than Gene and left home on the day she turned eighteen. Gene was devastated. A few years later, she returned when her father died. I guess they inherited a lot of money. Cheryl became the queen of the manor, but then she was always her father's favorite. She got to the point where she would hardly speak to her old friends. Gene went away to school a few months later, but there was a wedge there now. Only recently has he returned after all these years, and it's been so good seeing the two of them together. You can see the love there as strong as before, and Cheryl is acting more like the old Cheryl."

"I didn't know any of that, especially about my aunt and uncle," I said. "That is so sad. Life can be so hard on children, but at least they had each other back then for support. I guess the physical separation became an emotional one for them. The two of them are devoted to each other now, though. At every opportunity, Cheryl brags about how good Gene is to her."

"Yes, I saw them together in town one day. It was like they'd never been apart. Cheryl actually crossed the street to speak to me. I felt bad when I recalled those words that Josh heard, and I couldn't pull back. But I kid you not, Emma, that was a different Cheryl Pratt back then. Did you know her well?"

"Not since we were kids, but with hindsight, I was allowed to turn feral when I was with them. We ran wild as a troop of monkeys. It was quite an adjustment for me when I returned home."

We paddled back to my house and arrived with plenty of time for Cathy to pick up Crab from school. We pulled the kayaks from the water, and she helped me place them back in the racks attached to my Amish-built shed.

"I hope you enjoyed the trip, Cathy. If you want to go again, and you're game, we'll paddle out to the inlet and back."

"I loved it, Emma. It was so peaceful, and yes, I'll be back. Do you have slots open around the same time once a week?"

Chapter Nineteen

Sam hadn't arrived at the house yet, and it was too early to start dinner. The striped bass I'd picked up at the fish market was on the menu and wouldn't take long to cook. The mystery novel I'd left outside on the porch rocker caught my eye, and I curled up to read a few chapters.

It was a fast-paced read, but my lack of sleep took its toll. After the heroine had discovered the final puzzle clue but before the murderer's reveal, I had succumbed. My dreams were fragmented but upbeat. I walked through fields of flowers, and calm, crystal-clear waterways beckoned me.

I was reluctant to open my eyes, but when I did, Maya and Frank Pratt were there.

"You have to help them," Maya said. Her eyes were dark and sunken, as one might expect when talking to the dead, but never with Maya or, at least, never before.

"Who is they? What's wrong, Maya?"

"They need your help, or there will be another."

"Another what? Another murder, you mean?"

Frank stepped forward. His eyes were wide under a furrowed brow, and his lips quivered as he spoke.

"Help my Cheryl," he said. "She doesn't deserve this. Clear my name, Emma."

"I will. I know she didn't do what they are saying

about her. And I heard how you turned your life around, Frank. I'm doing all I can," I answered.

"You have all you need. You just need to open your eyes," Maya said.

****

"Who is this Frank?" Sam's voice asked. "Should I be jealous?"

I shook my head. "Sam, what are you doing here?"

"You invited me, Emma, remember? Open your eyes."

"Yes, open your eyes, Maya said. Must see."

Something tickled my foot, and I bolted up from the porch swing.

"Sam, what are you doing here?"

"I think we covered that already. Are you okay, Emma?"

"I'm sorry—weirdest dream. This case is weighing heavily on me, Sam. It has me confused. I can't get past the feeling that we have all the pieces if we can just put them together."

"We will get a break soon, and Cheryl is home now."

We enjoyed a beautiful sunset together. Sam poured us two glasses of homemade pear wine. It was comfortingly romantic, but the evening air still felt chilled in late Spring. After giving Sam a half-hearted admonishment or two about disturbing a girl while sleeping, we went inside.

I spiced our fish with seafood seasoning and popped it in the oven. Some freshly baked bread from Kat's and a can of sweet corn from my garden would round out our repast.

"Hello? Earth to Emma? You there, love?" Sam

asked.

"Did you say something?"

"I just wanted to know if I could help. You seem far away tonight."

"I was wondering about the etymology of the word crypt."

"Huh?" Sam scratched his head. "What did you decide?"

"I think it came about because ghosts are so dang cryptic. What do you think?"

"I think you need some sleep, Emma. Maybe we should turn in early tonight."

I nodded in agreement, but once we'd eaten and the dishes were done, my mind returned to the dream.

"I think I should call Cheryl to see how she is, Sam. Then there's a pie in the fridge if you want to make us a couple of decafs to go along with it."

"The blueberry?"

I nodded and smiled. Sam had a well-developed sweet tooth. Then, I sat on the couch to call. Gene answered.

"Hi, Gene. How are you guys making out? Has Cheryl settled down after her awful experience?"

"I think so, poor thing. I feel so sorry for her. She's gone through so much."

"And you've been at her side through it all, Cousin."

"Thanks for saying that, Emma, but it's also a blessing for me. Coming back home has been like finding a long-lost best friend. But give me a sec, and I'll get her for you. I'll warn you, though—she's been hitting the wine."

I heard the phone being placed on a table and the

soft notes of distant music before Cheryl picked up.

"Emma, Emma, Emma! Good evenin', my girl. How's it shakin'?"

"Cheryl? Are you all right? You sound…"

"Eneb—enerbe—eneberee—drunk? Gene 'n me been sipping wine—talkin' 'bout the old days."

I bit my lip, but laughter bubbled over in my voice. "I was worried about you, but it seems Gene has you in good spirits."

'Spirits." She laughed. "Tha's a good 'un. It was wine, though, Emmy. No hard stuff for this girl."

"That's great, Cheryl, that you're feeling better. I'll drop in on you tomorrow. Is there a good time?"

"I'll be here alllll day—not gone nowhere. I got my new ankle jewry, ya know."

We said our goodbyes as Sam walked in with a tray holding two plates and cups.

"Did you have her on speaker?" he asked.

"No, why?"

"Because of how loud her voice was coming through the phone. It sounded like she and Gene were hitting the bottle hard."

"Cheryl did, for sure. Gene either holds his booze better, or she needed it more. She probably will regret it in the morning, though. Cheryl never was much of a drinker," I said.

"Did I hear you say you were going over there tomorrow? Tell her if I can do anything to help, I'll…"

"She knows, Sam. Don't let Gene's tantrum at the restaurant weigh on you, but I'll be sure to tell her."

He kissed me on the forehead and dug into his pie.

Sleep came easy and fast that night. I slept until the neighbor's rooster perched outside my window and noisily announced a new dawn. I sat up as Sam was slipping on his shoes.

"I never asked last night, as we both had too much on our minds, but how did the kayaking trip go? What did you think of Cathy Grimes?"

"It went great, and I like Cathy a lot. My one or two old friends I've alienated lately. Everyone else in town still treats me like an outsider. Standoffish, you know? But you know how the county is—xenophobic is the word. All new arrivals are treated distantly for a few years. After my time away, my 'time-in-county' must have started all over again. I'm seen as a new arrival and not to be trusted. It was different with Cathy. She was honest and open with me. It was like talking with an old friend."

"Well, there is the Crab connection," Sam said.

"True, but I think we will be friends. She's also signed up for a kayaking excursion every week, so we'll see a lot of each other."

Sam left, and a shower and two cups of coffee later, the Bronco and I headed to Cheryl's house.

****

Something didn't feel right as soon as I pulled up in front of the house. The air was thick under a grey, cloudy sky that threatened rain.

I looked around carefully. Nothing looked amiss, but a girl learns to trust her instincts, and my senses tingled. I went up the front steps and saw that the door was cracked open. I reached behind my back to feel the comforting outline of the 9mm in my waistband.

"Cheryl? Gene!" I shouted and listened. No one answered, and there were no sounds of footfalls approaching.

I yelled out for my cousins again, but once more, no response. I snatched my phone and called Sam, but he didn't answer either, so I left a message: *"At Cheryl's. Something is wrong. No answer at the door. I hope she is OK. Call me!"*

I yelled out again, adding that I was coming in. At the threshold of each interior door, I called out their names. Where could they be? I searched the kitchen and dining rooms. An empty pair of wine bottles, two glasses, a spoon, and a soiled napkin were on the dining room table. I spotted a small white pill on Cheryl's spotless stone floor. It looked like an aspirin, but I shoved it into my pocket—just in case it meant something.

The living room was deserted, but something caught my eye under the far end of the couch. It looked like a cell phone, and I reached under to pull it out. It was Cheryl's ankle monitor!

My phone buzzed in my pocket—Sam.

I accepted the call, and Sam was already talking. "Emma, don't go in that house—"

"Sam, I—"

"Hold it right there, Mrs. Pratt," a male voice said behind me. "Drop what you're holding and put your hands in the air."

I dropped my phone and the ankle bracelet. I could hear Sam yelling.

"Turn around slowly, Mrs. Pratt," he said.

"I'm not Cheryl Pr…"

"Tell it to the judge." If the badge on his chest wasn't authority enough, the 9mm semi-automatic pointed at my chest was. He was a tall, flat-faced man with broad shoulders and a shaved head. He looked as if he could wrestle a bull moose to a draw.

"Officer, if you'll just—"

"On your knees. Hands behind your back, please, ma'am."

I complied, and he snatched the pistol from my waistband.

"Do you have a permit for this, ma'am?"

"I do." The cuffs tightened around my wrists. "Okay, Officer, I am subdued and, obviously, not a threat to you. Will you please pick up that phone and talk to my boyfriend, Major Sam Mattingley?"

"Yes, ma'am, I will when you sit on the couch where I can keep an eye on you."

I sat, and Officer Humungous picked up my phone. I could still hear Sam yelling on the other end, but not the words. What followed was a one-sided conversation for me.

"St. Merriam's County Parole Officer James Cummings speaking. Who am I speaking with, sir or ma'am?"

"That is correct, Deputy Mattingley—yes, Major Mattingley…"

Officer Cummings held the phone slightly away from his ear and licked his lips, then answered, "The monitoring company received two false alarms from this address last night, Major. Our officers investigated on both occasions and verified the detainee was on site. A third alarm was triggered two hours ago during the monitoring company's shift change."

The man's face flushed at Sam's next tirade.

"No, Major. It was not reported to my group in a timely fashion. I arrived fifteen minutes ago at zero-nine-thirty. I found the detainee with the cut ankle monitor in hand, attempting to escape."

Whatever was said next, the officer took the phone from his ear and turned toward me.

"Ma'am, do you have identification on your person?"

"No, but I do in my purse in the Bronco."

"Would you follow me, ma'am?" he asked.

I stood, and he led me out the front door by the elbow. At the Bronco's door, he asked, "Ma'am, do I have your permission to enter your vehicle and obtain your identification from your handbag?"

"Yes, it's in my wallet."

Cummings retrieved it. He stared at my driver's license, then at me, then both again.

"Miss Love, I apologize for the inconvenience. I hope you understand how it looked?" He handed me my phone.

"Emma, are you there? Are you okay?"

"Cheryl's gone, Sam! What was she thinking?"

"Is Gene there?"

"Nowhere to be seen. His sports car and Cheryl's caddy are both gone, too. Maybe Gene went after her, or Cheryl ran off when he went out for something?"

"There's already an arrest warrant out for Cheryl. I'm asking every available deputy to be on the lookout for Gene. He may have some idea. What color and model was his vehicle?"

"It's a cherry red two-seater. I don't know the make."

"Do you need me there, Emma?"

"No, I'm good—a little shaky, but I'm going straight home as soon as the officer gives me my firearm back. Please find her, Sam."

Chapter Twenty

I was ready to leave, but I poked around outside the house. Mashed grass marked a vehicle's progress to the backyard. A vehicle had parked behind the house, and the width was too narrow for either of their cars.

Two deputies, Joyce and Douglas, pulled up in their cruiser, and the parole officer repeated most of what he'd told Sam earlier.

"Miss Love, why are you still here?" Joyce asked. "The major said you would be, though. He said, and I quote, 'Tell her to get her butt home.' No offense meant, ma'am."

"None taken, Joyce. I have a group coming over to kayak this afternoon, anyway. I want to show you the tracks to the backyard before I go. Neither of the siblings ever parked back there, so it might be worth noting. They were obstinate about where they parked and irritated if a guest took their spot."

"I guess we all have our quirks. Do you think it means anything?"

"I don't know. Probably nothing, but maybe something to file in the back of our heads."

We walked the yard's perimeter, and Deputy Joyce and Douglas measured the tracks. I described where I found the ankle bracelet, the wine, and the glasses.

"Any wine left in the bottles or glasses?" Joyce asked.

"Ounces maybe at the most," I said. "I think they were hitting it pretty good last night."

Deputy Joyce nodded. "Okay. The major said we're treating this as a parole violation and looking for anything to aid in apprehending the escapee, but we were to leave no stone unturned."

"I'll bag the bottles and the glasses, then," Douglas said. "The major might want the wine tested. You know he likes to cross all the t's and dot all the i's."

****

Once home, I tried calling Sam but got no answer. Since I had no new information to pass along, I didn't leave a message. I hated to think what the day ahead would bring for him. I fixed myself a fried bologna sandwich for an early lunch and sat at the dining room table. By the second bite, my mind was whirling, and I couldn't sit still any longer. Where would Cheryl run to?

I texted Sam, —*Please update me when you find out anything.*— I went to my bedroom and carried my laptop back to the table. Researching the morning departure times from the bus and train stations, I jotted down all the departures from this morning. I also investigated the DCA airport departures, but there were too many to search, and I was sure the police all-points bulletin would have that covered.

I rubbed my temples. It had been a stressful morning. Searching my medicine cabinet for relief reminded me of what I found on Cheryl's dining room floor. I dug in my pocket and examined the pill. The tablet was engraved with "KET/200."

Another online query identified it for what it was. Ketamine was described as a club drug, otherwise known as a date rape drug. No way that it was Cheryl's. I always suspected Gene might suffer from odd proclivities, but this was a bit much. Was it possible they were kidnapped?

I called Sam again, and once again, my call went to voicemail.

"Sam, I'm sorry, but I just remembered; I picked up a pill off Cheryl's floor. Yes, I know better. The heat of the moment, ya know? Anyway, it's ketamine. Call me back when you can. I'll drop it off at the station later."

I tried Cheryl's and Gene's phone numbers. I wasn't surprised when neither one answered.

I finished my sandwich and washed my dish and glass. When I checked my phone, I saw no response from Sam, but its sudden ring startled me.

"Miss Love? This is Jimmy Hill."

"Hi, Jimmy. Are we still on for kayaking this afternoon? Two couples, you said?"

"Well, that's why I'm calling, ma'am. I'm afraid we need to cancel today's trip. My little girl, Felicity, is home sick from school today, and the wife is keeping an eye on her."

"Is she doing okay?"

"She has a bit of a fever, but after her bout with the flu last year, we aren't taking any chances. I realize the deposit is non-refundable…"

"Nonsense, Jimmy. I require a deposit to make sure I get genuinely interested clients, not to punish parents of sick children. I can reimburse you or retain it toward another date. Your choice."

"That would be wonderful, Miss Love. I will contact you to reschedule as soon as Felicity is on the mend. Bob and Sally are looking forward to it, too."

When Jimmy disconnected, I smiled. It hurt to lose the money from my scheduled outing, but now, my afternoon was free.

I remembered our foray to the bail bondsman on Louse Alley and the unsavory characters there. I began a text to Sam but changed my mind and slid the phone into my pocket. I didn't think he'd approve of my plans, and he had enough on his plate. He didn't need to worry about me as well. Grabbing my purse, I headed for the door. My ever-faithful steed (the Bronco) was waiting.

En route to Newtowne, I passed by three sheriff's cruisers heading in the opposite direction. Their lights weren't flashing, so I doubted they'd located Cheryl. Maybe Gene?

I slowed as I approached the turnoff through Louse Alley. I stared down the narrow street and spied the object of my quest, but a different man now slouched against the light pole, smoking. He appeared in no hurry to go anywhere. He didn't look at all like the stereotypical and clichéd drug dealer from before. He looked more like a fresh Army recruit with his crewcut blond hair and camouflage shirt. His jeans were clean and pressed. He looked more of an outsider here than I did. When visiting the bondsman, though, I noticed his associate salesman's subtle transactions at that corner with the cars that stopped and then hurried away. I knew what he was.

Parking on Main Street, I felt for my 9 mm when I left the car (a gal can't be too careful in that neighborhood) and strutted toward him as if it was an everyday occurrence for me. The last thing I wanted was to appear nervous or out of place.

He flashed hyper-white teeth in a wide smile as I drew nearer.

"Hey, hey, sweet lady. What can ol' Numba One do for you taday?"

"You can speak normally with me, Skipper. Yeah, I know who you are. You don't need the street cred with me. I babysat you and changed a few of your dirty diapers."

"You a cop?"

"No, but my boyfriend is the lead deputy sheriff. I can get him here in two shakes."

He held up his hands, palms out.

"Hey, hey now. No need for all that. What do you want, lady?"

I reached into my pocket and pulled out the tablet from Cheryl's. I held it up inches from his face.

"Do you know what this is, Skip?"

He shrugged his shoulders. "I ain't no pharmacist. How'd I know?"

"Okay, if that's how you want to play this." I pulled out my phone again.

"Whoa, now, lady. No need for all that. It's Special K. What's a nice lady like you doing with that?"

"Do you sell this stuff, Skip?"

"Who, me?"

"I know your mother, too, Skip."

"Okay, lady, geez. I won't say I do if you understand my meaning. but I know folks who do. It's not in much demand, ya know."

"I want you to look at a picture and tell me if you have ever had dealings with the other two people in it." I handed him my phone open to a selfie of Gene, Cheryl, and me. He stared at the picture and then back at me.

"Hey, aren't you one of the Loves from up on the hill?" Skipper asked.

"Kind of, it's my brother's place. The picture?"

"Yeah, I know the man on there, but not her. Bet she was a looker back in the day."

"So, he was a customer? What did you sell to him?" I asked.

"Now wait, Miss Love. I didn't say anything about selling anything, but a friend of a friend told me the man in the picture bought a half-dozen Special K like you flashed in my face."

****

I was on the way to the sheriff's office when Sam's call came through. I pulled the Bronco over to the shoulder of the road.

"Have you found Cheryl, Sam?"

"No, and hello to you, too, Emma."

"Sorry. Is there nothing new, then?"

"Well, we did find Gene's car. It was parked behind the church. One of the parishioners reported it. The driver's side window was broken out."

"It was broken into? What do you think happened? Was he working at the church for some reason? Did anyone notice lights on in the church last night?"

"Not that we have found. I thought he might have been retrieving something that Frank had left there. Otherwise, I don't know what to think. But either they're on the run, or someone abducted them both," Sam said. "Are you aware of anyone who might have a grudge against either or both of them?"

"Kat, maybe. She had a reason to hate them both, but that wasn't the feeling I got from her. When I get home, I'll scroll through "NeighborSnoop" to see what I can find out."

"What was between them and Katrina?" Sam asked.

"It's a long story, but I'm about two minutes away from you to drop off the pill from Cheryl's house."

"Yes. about that, Emma..." Sam started.

"See you in a minute," I said and disconnected.

When I arrived, Sam was on the phone and waved through the plate glass window. Finding Deputy Douglas down the hall, I passed the pill to him.

"I have a favor to ask, Douglas. Do you think I could see the evidence in the Pratt/Johnson murder cases?"

"Umm, I don't know, Emma. That would have to be cleared by the sheriff, and he's on a doctor's visit. The major could approve it, but he just got through to someone he's been trying to reach for hours, so he might be a while." Douglas shrugged.

"You know I've seen most of it anyway. How about if I don't touch anything without gloves, and you guard me? I promise to be quick."

"What do you hope to find?" he asked.

"I just thought an extra set of eyes—maybe I could pick up on something."

Douglas glanced through Sam's office window and saw Sam alternating between attentive listening and animated responses. He shook his head and nodded toward the end of the hall. Pulling a set of keys from the wall, he opened the door to the furthest room. He led me between the rows of shelving and stopped in front of a series of boxes labeled Pratt/Johnson with the date it was initiated and the case number.

Douglas carried one box to a corner table and dumped it. Inside were the contents of the picnic basket discovered at the scene. Someone had added the rifle casings from the creek bank, but everything else I'd seen before.

"Thanks, Douglas, would you mind getting one of the others?"

Douglas put on blue surgical-style gloves and gathered the items from box one. He carried it back to the shelf and returned with another. It was filled with recovered trash items, half-eaten food, and the personal effects of the deceased. The third box, likewise, held no surprises.

"I really appreciate this, Douglas," I said as he dumped the fourth and final evidence box.

"Yes, ma'am."

He spread the items on the table again, and something immediately caught my eye.

"What is that? Would you pick it up for me, please?"

"It's the poison spoon," he said.

"What do you mean by the poison spoon? Was it from Cheryl's potting shed?"

"No, not from the shed. This is the spoon that was in the bakery inside the jelly bucket that held the poison."

"This is the same pattern of cutlery as Cheryl has at her home. There was a spoon on the table at her house this morning. Did you bag it?"

"We bagged everything on her table."

"Thank you, Douglas. No wonder her prints were on it."

"I'm sorry. What did you say, Emma?"

"Never mind, but thank you, Douglas. I appreciate it. Would you tell Sam about this, though? And that I'll see him at home? Thank you."

On the way home, I wondered if recognizing the spoon would help or hurt Cheryl's case. I went to my computer as soon as I got there. I hoped to find something that might help to see where Cheryl could be—assuming she went of her own volition. A kidnapping seemed improbable, yet it was the only thing that made sense to me. There is no way Cheryl would have sacrificed her home and her life to avoid a trial for something she was innocent of. And she had to be innocent. *But what if she wasn't?*

Chapter Twenty-One

I opened the "NeighborSnoop" site and started searching. I'd just started digging into old records from the Love family—the other side of the family. It didn't feel right, like looking through a neighbor's window. I was an Internet peeping Tom, but it had to be done. I had to get my hands dirty again.

Before I got into any of the murky details, I heard a car in need of a muffler pulling into my driveway. I peeked out of the kitchen window and spotted the familiar jet-black "mini hearse" belonging to Johnny Walker. I hated to turn him away, but it had to be done.

Taking a quick step to my door, he hopped up the steps and knocked three times. I considered sitting quietly and ignoring him, hoping he'd go away. I knew he'd seen my Bronco parked in plain sight, and I couldn't be so rude. My mother would roll over in her grave, and Johnny was also a friend.

I opened the door a crack and peered out.

"Hi, Johnny. What brings you here?"

"Remember, I mentioned needing to talk with you? I really must, Emma. If you'll…"

"This is not a good time, Johnny. I promise I will do the interview with you soon, but I must get through this case with Cheryl first—"

"This is about the case, Emma. I must speak to you about it." Johnny answered, and the sincerity in his eyes was not to be denied.

"Come on in then, Johnny. Can I get you a cup of coffee or something else?"

"A tall glass of water would be nice, thank you, Emma. I have a lot to tell you, but I promise it won't take long."

I unconsciously glanced at my watch as I retrieved a glass for Johnny.

"Give me five minutes, and if you don't want to hear any more. I'll scoot," Johnny said.

"I'm not a very good hostess, Sorry."

"No need to be sorry, Emma. I practically pushed my way in, but I think it's important."

I put two glasses of water down in front of us and sat beside him.

"Okay, Johnny, what's this all about?"

"It's mostly about your cousin Gene. I didn't know he was your cousin at first, or I would've told you before. He said he wasn't from the local Love family and that he was from up in Connecticut. I didn't know until I saw you there that day. I was surprised, and then when he…"

"Whoa, Johnny, slow down. You knew Gene before all this went down?" I asked, and Johnny took a deep breath.

"Remember when I came back to work for *The County Examiner*?" he asked.

"Yes, you said the new editor who hired you offered you a raise and…"

"Yeah, but it was Gene. Gene Love is the new editor. He was the guy who interviewed me over a month ago. So, he has been at the paper since…"

"Since before Pastor Frank or Marsha Johnson

were killed?"

"Right. Why would he say he wasn't related to your family?" Johnny asked.

"I have no clue. When did you realize who he was?" I asked.

"I saw him at the Pratts' house that morning when the cops arrested Cheryl Pratt."

"That's why you left when he waved you off?"

"Sure, he was the boss. After that, I did some digging. I discovered who he was and how long he'd been in the area. He was camped out at that historic Newtowne motel for over two months. That's where he had me meet him for my interview, too. You know the place? I think they rent rooms by the hour."

"I'm familiar with it. Never had the displeasure of staying there." I took a slow drink of water while my brain sorted the new information. I had so many questions.

"Knowing all that, why would Gene, as the editor, allow that journalist to write up those two hit pieces on Cheryl?"

"Well, that is another thing I wanted to tell you, but it is just conjecture on my part. That woman, Suzanne Abbot? She doesn't exist," Johnny said.

"What do you mean? Of course, she does."

"Nobody at the paper has ever met her. Nobody has even heard of her. I have a friend in accounting. She says no check or online payment has been sent to anyone by that name, including outside vendors, freelance contributors, or repairmen, just nobody. She doesn't exist."

"Then who wrote her pieces?" I asked.

"Remember, this is conjecture, but I believe

Suzanne Abbot is Gene Love's pseudonym. Suzanne Abbot is Gene Love, and he wrote those stories."

"If he sold out his sister, what else did he do?" I asked.

"And why?" Johnny added.

****

Johnny stayed for another half an hour as we discussed everything he had shared. He talked about the newspaper's office politics and gossip about their editor's disappearance. When the conversation slowed, and we were lost in our thoughts, he stood to leave. I thanked him for the information and his friendship and then walked him to the door. He admired the sunset over the bay as we said our goodbyes. I promised to get with him on our interview within the following week, rain or shine.

I carried my portable radio out to the porch and tuned it to the local station, but I was too late to hear any updates on Cheryl and Gene. They'd already moved on to the weather. The throaty sound of Sam's Mustang outside assured me I wouldn't have much longer to wait.

I yelled as he stepped out, "Hey, handsome. I almost forgot tomorrow is your day off until I saw you'd swapped your cruiser for the Mustang."

"Well, it will be a no-pay day, but you know I'll be working on finding Cheryl anyway."

"A busman's holiday, huh? Well, it will be a project we work on together. I have a lot to tell you that Johnny Walker told me."

"Me too, and you can go first. I grabbed some eats from the Mexican restaurant in town. Do you want to share Johnny's story while we eat? After dinner, I have a tape for you to listen to."

I had carnitas, and Sam had the restaurant's special Tres Amigos. We ate as if it were our last meal or the first in a while. Between wolf-sized bites, I ran down everything that Johnny Walker had revealed.

"This ties in with what I found out today, and it shoots down any thoughts about kidnapping. This had to be planned."

"I agree, but I don't think Cheryl was involved in the planning. What would Gene's motive be?" I asked.

"I did some research on Gene and discovered his last employer. I finally reached him and asked what he could tell me. After some hemming and hawing about privacy concerns, he opened up. He said Gene was not very social and made very few friends at the paper, but gave me the name of Todd Warren as the best source. Warren was described as having somewhat of a relationship with Gene." Sam stood, walked to the hallway table, and retrieved his pocket-sized recorder. He put it on the table between us.

"This is the recording of my conversation with the man," he said and pressed 'play.'

"Mr. Warren, this is Major Mattingley of the St. Merriam's Sheriff's Department. I have some questions about one of your former colleagues, Gene Love."

"If I can help, officer. I didn't know the man very well, though. We grabbed a few beers after work on occasion."

"Excellent, Mr. Warren. Do I have your permission to record our conversation?"

"I don't have any problem with that," he answered.

"I am particularly interested in anything he might have shared about his financial situation and his relationship with his family," Sam explained.

"Ah, is someone finally coming after Love for nonpayment of a debt? The man was constantly poor-mouthing. If I was lucky, he might spring for one round out of three—on a good night. He blamed all that on his family, as well as every misfortune he'd had in life. I don't know what happened there, but he was bitter."

"Did he ever mention why?" Sam asked.

"Not that I recall, but he hated his old man. I believe they were from somewhere down in the southern part of Maryland. Is that where you are located, Major?"

"It is. We say it is the furthest south you can go in Maryland without getting your feet wet."

"Gene had a sister, too, as I recall," the man added. "He couldn't stand her either."

"Were you surprised when he took the job on the paper down here?"

"Was I surprised when he did? Heck, I'm surprised now. We all thought he was on a two-week vacation. So, he's working down there now? What is he doing?"

"Gene is the new editor for *The County Examiner* newspaper."

"An editor's job? Are we talking about the same Gene Love? That paper must be hard-pressed for help. Gene never bothered to fact-check his own stories. His grammar was worse than mine, and I failed eighth-grade English. My editor fixes the worst mistakes, and she claims that my writing style connects with the common man. That doesn't make me an editor, though."

"Did anything happen at the paper that would have pushed Gene to move home? Was he in danger of being laid off, or did he lose a promotion?" Sam asked.

"No, not that I'm aware of. The last thing Gene said to me along those lines was that he'd never move back there and hoped he never saw the place again, even in his nightmares."

"Thank you, Mr. Warren. The department appreciates your cooperation. Can we contact you again if there are any additional questions?"

"Any time, Major. You have my number."

****

The recording went silent. Sam hit the 'stop' button and turned to me.

"What do you think, Emma?"

"He took her, Sam."

"But why and where?"

"Based on what you got from Mr. Warren, I think we can figure that out," I said, reaching for my laptop on the kitchen counter.

"Don't tell me. Is it—"

"Yup, it's time for 'NeighborSnoop.'"

"I still haven't investigated that site to see if it's even legal," Sam said.

"That's probably best." I smiled.

"What is the search criteria?"

"The last will and testament of Gene Love, Senior."

The results would have surprised me if not for the comments by Todd Warren. Gene Jr. was mentioned first in his father's will after all the 'of sound mind and body parts':'

'To my only son, Gene Junior, in appreciation for the less than stellar care in his sister's absence, I leave the uneaten canned soups he provided for my daily fare and the opened bottle of twenty-year-old bourbon in the cabinet. On his road of entitlement, it may be his only source of comfort in the coming years. I hope it will encourage him to make a man of himself, and one day he will thank me.'

I looked back at Sam, who was reading over my shoulder.

"Wow, I know you said Cheryl was always his favorite, but what a terrible way to treat your own flesh and blood," Sam said.

I nodded and read on:

'To my daughter, Cheryl, I leave the remainder of my worldly possessions with the caveat that she moves back here to her ancestral home.'

We looked at each other and shook our heads.

"Not much of a father," Sam said.

"I don't know much of Cheryl's life when she moved away, but he didn't give her much choice. She had to move home or forfeit everything. Crab's mother, Cathy Grimes, said Cheryl had a dark time around then."

"No wonder Gene was so bitter," Sam said. "I'm afraid for Cheryl. How far would he go, do you think?"

"We have to find her, Sam."

Chapter Twenty-Two

So many puzzle pieces were fighting for position in our minds, and none wanted to fit in place. I thought of Leo, our family's puzzle master, since he was a toddler. That thought was all that brought a smile to my face.

After tossing ideas off one another, we made no progress and decided to call it a night. An early start in the morning would give us fresh perspectives.

Sam was asleep in minutes. His nasal snores and my brain that would not shut up kept me staring at the walls until the wee hours. I was afraid my tossing and turning would wake him. I slipped out of bed and curled up on the couch with my mystery novel. I knew I was close to nodding off when I had to reread the same paragraph three times.

My dream and my novel joined forces in my sleep. I stood in front of the door that, in my book, held the final clue. I pulled it open, and I was outside with Maya.

I recognized it at once. The river stretched before me, and the sweet, tangy smell of salt water filled my nose. Behind Maya was the small cabin Uncle Gene owned.

"Why are you here, Maya? You never came here with us."

"You don't remember, Sis? Well, you weren't bigger than a minute," she said.

Cheryl and young Gene ran across the sand toward us. I never remembered them so young. I looked at my hands. They were pudgy toddler hands.

"Little Emmy girl, do you want to get in the water with me?" Cheryl asked in a sugar-sweet voice reserved for speaking to the very young.

"Eww, not me," Gene said, turning up his nose. "There's jellyfish in there."

"Listen, Em," Maya said. I heard an outboard motor starting and watched it zoom across the Potomac, throwing up a rooster tail wake.

My eyes flew open.

"Crab said Gene rented a boat!" I shouted. "The tracks at the house were from a boat trailer!"

I heard a thump in the bedroom, and Sam ran out wrapped in a blanket.

"Emma, are you all right?" he asked.

"I need a Potomac River map, and we need a boat, Sam. I know where they are, and I believe Cheryl is in trouble."

Sam dug through my catch-all drawer in the hutch until he located the river map. I spread it out on the coffee table in front of the couch.

"There it is," I said, pointing at the map.

"It? What is that?" Sam asked.

"It's a creek off the river by Nomini Bay. It's where Uncle Gene had his cabin years ago. That must be where they are. I thought it odd that Gene rented a boat from Crab's father's marina. It has to be where they are. Gene was never one for the water. He is pure landlubber."

"Nomini Bay is Virginia waters, Emma. I have no jurisdiction there," Sam said.

"I don't care, Sam. There's no time. They will have to catch up. Cheryl needs us. We can worry about the paperwork later."

Sam called to ask Douglas to trailer the skiff to us and to inform Virginia authorities.

"No, I don't have the coordinates. It's a small creek on the northern edge of Nomini Bay past Shark Tooth Island. I'll send coordinates when I get to the mouth of the creek. See you in five minutes."

I dressed and headed for the door.

"Douglas isn't here yet," Sam said.

"It's low tide," I said. "We need to tow the two-seater kayak behind us. That creek is shallow. We won't be able to run the skiff in there, and a sandbar stretches out from the island, too. Besides, we'll want to go in quiet."

Sam helped me tote the kayak to the dock as we heard a powerboat approach. As it drew near, Deputy Douglas waved.

"Ready, Major? The sheriff thought this would be quicker than trailering the other skiff over. He said for me to go and keep you out of trouble."

I tied the kayak to the stern, and Sam and I climbed aboard. The skiff roared across the bay and into the Potomac.

"Straight across to Nomini," Sam said.

****

"It's there," I yelled, pointing. "That's the creek."

Douglas cut back on the throttle, and we floated until the boat's hull bottomed out. "Major, we better pull up the outboard, or we'll be dredging mud."

Sam pulled the prop out of the water while I untied the kayak.

"Stay with the boat, Emma," Sam said. "Douglas and I will take the kayak in,"

"That is not happening, Major Deputy Sam Mattingley," I said. "Cheryl is my family, and I will go even if I have to swim."

"I think the lady is serious, Douglas," Sam said.

"Yes, sir. I'll man the boat."

****

The creek was shallow, as every stroke struck the paddle-sucking muddy bottom.

"How much farther in is it, Em?" Sam asked. "We'll need to get out and drag the kayak soon."

"A hundred yards, maybe, and this is as shallow as it gets for a while. It's on higher ground past a big stand of wild asparagus. We used to pick it when we were kids."

Cattails encroached on the edges of the creek. I pointed to the tendrils of asparagus poking up their heads, and then we spotted the rental boat. Grimes Marina was stenciled on the side with the Maryland license number below the wording.

"How did he get that back in here?" Sam whispered.

"It's smaller than your skiff, so less draft to navigate the shallow waters. Probably high tide when they came in, too," I said.

We pulled the kayak out of the creek and into the reeds. No one would see it until they were on top of it.

"Keep your head down, Emma. We can get to the cabin wading low in the water, and we won't be seen."

Five yards closer, then ten—the cabin was thirty yards away when...

"Help! Help me! Somebody! Help! Oh, please

help!" The screams echoed over the water, sending shorebirds flying in a whirl of wings and splashing water.

We dashed out of the water and up the bank to the cabin. Sam tried the door, but it was locked. He backed up and threw his shoulder against it. Screws popped from the hinges, but the door held. I heard a motorboat starting below us. It sounded close.

"Is someone there?" Cheryl's voice rang out. "Help me, please!"

Sam backed up again and slammed into the door. The hinges popped free, and he tumbled forward to the floor.

Cheryl was perched on a small, wobbly barstool, her feet overhanging its edge. Her legs were shaking, and a noose circling her neck reached up to the exposed rafters.

"Emma, help me. I can't—I can't stand here much longer."

"We're here, Cheryl. Hold on."

Her legs began to shake like an animal in its death throes. "Please, Emma!"

I reached for a rustic footstool to stand on. I picked it up as Cheryl's barstool skittered across the floor.

I heard my primal scream fill the air, even as Sam snatched her up and held her aloft.

"I've got her, Emma. Get the noose off her," Sam said.

****

Cheryl and I paddled the kayak while Sam waded through the creek in front of us. Cheryl shared her story.

"I don't know how it happened, Emma. One

minute, Gene and I were sipping a glass of wine. He was so sweet in supporting me, telling me everything would be all right. The next thing I remember, we were racing across the water in someone's boat. I thought I was dreaming, and I must have passed out. My next memory was waking up on that nasty old cot in the cabin."

"Gene drugged you, Cheryl," I said.

"I figured he did, and more than once, I think. I was in and out all day yesterday. He made me a nice breakfast this morning. After we ate, he listened to his police scanner for a few minutes. Then he said something about it being time to pay the piper. That's when he got mean."

"Did he hurt you?" Sam asked.

"He told me to write a note telling people how sorry I was for being mean to them. I thought that was strange, but he said my sins would be forgiven if I did it, and he'd take me home."

"That's how he got you to write the suicide note we found?" I asked.

"Yes, in my confused state of mind—short and sweet: 'To whom it may concern, I'm so sorry for anyone I've mistreated. Sincerely, Cheryl Pratt.' After that, he slipped that rope around my neck, dragged me over to the stool, and made me climb up on it. He looped it over the rafters and tied it off. Then he said, 'Have a nice day. Sis. See you in Hades.'"

As we moved around the last turn before the river, Sam stopped and held his palm up for us to remain quiet.

"Cheryl, lie flat in the kayak like you're dead. Don't say a word."

Gene was straight ahead, his boat run aground in the shallows.

****

"Hey, Gene," Sam shouted out. "Are you stuck?"

"Sam Mattingley, is that you? What are you doing out here?"

"Emma wanted to show me where you came as kids, but we found something terrible."

"Oh? Is Cheryl okay? I just left to pick up some groceries. She didn't fall, did she? I told her I'd paint tomorrow and to stay off the ladder."

Sam reached the side of Gene's boat and held on.

"You might want to sit down, Gene. I'm afraid we have terrible news. It looks like Cheryl has killed herself."

Gene dropped theatrically into the boat seat, but a sliver of a smile curled the edge of his lips.

"Oh no, it can't be," he said.

Tears were shed as Sam comforted him. I thought they both deserved Academy Awards.

At one point, Cheryl stifled a sneeze, and I squeezed my nose.

"I hope you aren't getting a cold," Sam said. "I think we better get Emma back home, Gene and— Cheryl too."

I paddled the kayak, and Sam dragged Gene's boat through the creek. The boat's hull kept getting stuck in the mud bottom, but Gene never offered to get out to help. Finally, when the river was only feet away, Gene noticed the sheriff's skiff just offshore.

"What's he..." Gene started, and Sam gave the boat a massive shove, spilling him back in his seat.

The boat was entirely out in the river now, and

Sam smiled.

"Cheryl, you can sit up now. Gene Love, I'm hereby arresting you for murder, attempted murder, and kidnapping…"

"Hey, buddy, we're in Virginia. You can't touch me…"

"Actually, Gene, you are beyond the mean low tide level in the Potomac River. You are in Maryland waters now."

Sam read his rights and handcuffed Gene to the boat's steering wheel.

Chapter Twenty-Three

With Sheriff Wathen's blessing, Sam asked me to observe Gene's interrogation the next day. They let him stew in his juices overnight and told me to be on-site at noon. Gene's lawyer was already there, and I sat in front of a monitor where I could see and hear everything.

The lawyer looked fresh out of high school, and my first thought was that he was a public defender. I doubted Gene could afford much else, and I didn't see Cheryl footing the bill.

"I understand that you want to make a full confession, Gene. Is that accurate?" Sam asked.

The lawyer held up his finger and whispered in Gene's ear, then he nodded.

"My client is willing to cooperate if given a reduced sentence."

"I have spoken with the district attorney, and she stated there will be no plea bargaining in this case," Sam said. "She is willing to take the death penalty off the table and will advise the judge of the prisoner's cooperation. That is all."

The lawyer whispered in Gene's ear again.

"What difference does it make?" Gene spurted out. "They matched my fingerprints to the canoe and some of its contents. They have an eyewitness in my sister. Who knows what else? I am not a wealthy man—far from it. I begged and borrowed against everything to maintain that illusion in Newtowne. Do you really think you will get me off with a slap on the wrist?"

The lawyer whispered in his ear again.

"I didn't think so. Okay, what do you want to know, Sam, that you don't already know?" he asked.

"Tell us what you did and why you did it."

"They left me with nothing, my own father and sister! They disowned me and hung me out to dry. Cheryl gave me an allowance in college that left me a virtual pauper. I was living hand to mouth, working odd jobs between classes. I soon dropped out," Gene said.

"What did this drive you to do, Gene?"

"I think you can figure that out, Deputy."

"I need you to say it in your words, please."

"Fine. Yes, I broke into that bakery and planted the spoon from Cheryl's house—the house that should've been mine. I was the one left behind to care for that miserly, miserable old man," he said.

"Why at Katrina Baker's? Didn't you think about what that would do to her reputation and business?"

"Her friends are so blind; it didn't slow down her business at all. Her reputation I couldn't care less about. She wasn't as pure as the driven snow. Years ago, I was foolish enough to ask her to the prom. She flat-out refused me, then started dating that pretty boy Brian Nash. So, no, I didn't care if it looked bad for her or not, but Cheryl had to pay. I took out that goody-two-shoes reverend of hers and his side piece. That fool was planning to give her my money, too. I saw him draw it from the bank, though he didn't see me. Money that I never recovered, either. It was the perfect revenge. Cheryl took everything from me. I would do the same to her and take even more. I would finally get back what was rightfully mine."

"It didn't seem like you planned to allow your sister to live. You rented a boat a week back. What else did you plan to do with it if not take her to your father's cabin and kill her?" Sam asked.

"Not initially, I thought a life sentence would suffice. Eventually, I decided her demise would be best. The dead cannot defend themselves. I parked my car at the church and smashed out a window. I hoped it would confuse your boys long enough, and if one of their parishioners were blamed, it would be even better. I had a good story prepared about the two of us being kidnapped. You know I am a journalist, even if my credentials are forged. Ah, that made you smile, did it?"

"Thank you, Gene," Sam said. "I think we're done for now. Your statement will be typed out, and we'll bring it in for you to verify that it is as you stated. Do you have any questions?"

Gene shook his head, and Deputy Douglas entered to escort him to his cell.

Sam looked up at the camera and winked.

"Well done, Emma. Lunch?"

Epilogue

Few things are as rewarding as a case solved, and nothing is as sweet as seeing justice served. I hated to think of the cost, but the innocent were cleared, and the guilty were made to pay for their crimes. Still, something felt undone. What was missing?

The evening after Gene's confession, the feeling persisted, and sleep eluded me. In the middle of the night, I remembered what I'd promised Frank during my conversation with Maya. That was it. I knew what had to be done. I slept like a baby the rest of the night. In the morning, I called Johnny Walker and made an appointment with him for later in the day.

Frank Pratt had flaws, as do we all, but he strove to be virtuous. Johnny agreed to run an editorial clearing Frank's name and shaming the community for their condemnation of such a beloved, righteous man. As the new editor of *The County Examiner,* Johnny had latitude on what was published. In return for that favor, I gave him an interview on my process and the particulars of the case.

When I left Johnny's cottage on McIlhenny Creek, a black and white zebra-striped tabby approached me.

"What a pretty kitty. Is she yours?" I asked.

"No, not mine, but I've been feeding her. She won't let me get close enough to touch her or read the name on her collar," Johnny said.

I sat on the steps, and the kitty nuzzled her face against my leg.

"Wow, she likes you," Johnny said.

I gently scratched her neck, and she purred. I glanced at her collar. It read 'Misty,' Mrs. Abell's missing cat. I'd finally solved the case of the missing kitty with some help from my friends.

"Call of the Falconer" (Dystopian Novella)

"Haunted Southern Maryland" (Paranormal History)

"Haunted Potomac River Valley" (Paranormal History)

SHORT STORIES

'Possum Stew (Short Story Collection)

What If #2 (Anthology GBB Authors)

What If #3 (Anthology GBB Authors)

What If #4 (Anthology GBB Authors)

https://www.david-w-thompson.com/

Thank you for purchasing
this publication of The Wild Rose Press, Inc.

For questions or more information
contact us at
info@thewildrosepress.com.

The Wild Rose Press, Inc.
www.thewildrosepress.com